BUS STORIES

MAGGIE OAKS

authorHOUSE®

AuthorHouse™
1663 Liberty Drive
Bloomington, IN 47403
www.authorhouse.com
Phone: 1 (800) 839-8640

Published by AuthorHouse 08/07/2019

ISBN: 978-1-7283-2248-3 (sc)
ISBN: 978-1-7283-2246-9 (hc)
ISBN: 978-1-7283-2247-6 (e)

Library of Congress Control Number: 2019911325

Hebrews 10 :19-23 "Therefore, brothers, since we have confidence to enter the Most Holy Place by the blood of Jesus, 20 By a new and living way opened for us through the curtain, that is, His body, 21 And since we have a great priest over the house of God, 22 Let us draw near to God with a sincere heart in full assurance of faith, having our hearts sprinkled to cleanse us from a guilty conscience and having our bodies washed with pure water. 23 Let us hold unswervingly to the hope we profess, for He who promised is faithful."

A NEW AND LIVING WAY

I am full of awe how Heavenly Father is towards us. How wonderful He is.

Once more I caught the "late" #113 bus, after the sound of the "early" #113 had faded and the #1 bus came full. Sitting on the empty bus, I asked Heavenly Father if He had a scripture in mind. What was it He wanted to share today? At work, I read Hebrews 10, verses 19 to 23 seemed more pronounced than the rest. After, I read an email from a very wise woman whom I had asked to share what she did with me on Sunday. Tears came to my eyes and joy to my heart as they did on Sunday. You see, that wise woman is my daughter, it touched and blessed my heart to hear plus see her spiritual growth.

How much more is Heavenly Father's joy when He observes our, individual, discovery of each faction of that new and living way that He opened for us through His Son Jesus Christ, as He faithfully promised.

I hope you are blessed also by my daughter's sharing.

"I have heard this message before, in words other than this. I have heard this message, but never absorbed it. I have heard that I am to seek God. I know that I must pursue Him. But, just the other night, I heard it in a way that hit home. So often, when I pray, I ask God why? Why this? Why that? Why to virtually everything. I have read in the scripture that says I am not to ask my Maker why He created me. But still I ask. I push.

1

I persist. I ask who I am and what my purpose is, more often than not, without a reply. Then I heard Him say, "Why do you not ask me who I am? Why do you not ask what My purpose is?".

Suddenly, I imagined the day that I will stand before Him in front of the multitudes. I feared that He will say, "I never knew you". I asked myself if I really knew God. If I met Him face to face, would I recognize Him? Would I know His voice? So, I began to ask God to forgive me and then I asked Him who He was. I wasn't ready to ask Him for His purpose yet. Then I decided to flip open my Bible to whatever page it landed on and see what it would teach me. I read Ezekiel 15. I listed everything I could plainly see described Him on paper. After that, I felt led to list everything not plainly seen, what was between the lines. As I did this, I wandered back to my Bible into Chapter 16 and read until verse 15. It is an allegory of Jerusalem. He describes how He found her and how He cared for her and ultimately how she betrays Him. Then, I began to feel God's love. I began to remember my first love. I began to realize, I do know God. I know my Savior and what He has done for me. Again, I repented and I asked God if a day would ever come that I would not need reminders to stay focused. I asked if I would overcome, if I would be faithful in the end. Then I remembered a scene from one of my favorite movies, Lord of the Rings. Frodo announces to the counsel that he will take the ring to Mordor, though he does not know the way. It dawned on me that the ring is much like our flesh. Our life is a journey to destroy the ring, the flesh, the power struggle. The ring, our flesh, is a deception of great power. When, in reality, it is just bondage and it will indeed destroy us. Then, I began to see His purpose. I began to see how the pains and sufferings of life humble us so we can hear God. I thanked Him for His grace and His mercy. I thanked Him for His patience with me and I said, "I will take the journey, though I do not know the way." And I felt a great peace inside, that my Father knows. I need only follow Him."

God Bless,

Psalm 28: 1-9

1 To you I call, O LORD my Rock; do not turn a deaf ear to me. For if You remain silent, I will be like those who have gone down to the pit. 2 Hear my cry for mercy as I call to You for help, as I lift up my hands toward Your Most Holy Place. 3 Do not drag me away with the wicked, with those who do evil, who speak cordially with their neighbors but harbor malice in their hearts. 4 Repay them for their deeds and for their evil work; repay them for what their hands have done and bring back upon them what they deserve. 5 Since they show no regard for the works of the LORD and what His hands have done, He will tear them down and never build them up again. 6 Praise be to the LORD, for He has heard my cry for mercy.7 The LORD is my strength and my shield; my heart trusts in Him, and I am helped. My heart leaps for joy and I will give thanks to Him in song. 8 The LORD is the strength of His people, a fortress of salvation for His anointed one. 9 Save Your people and bless Your inheritance; be their Shepherd and carry them forever.

Feeling Blessed

Today, I feel extremely blessed. Nothing out of the extraordinary has happened, so far. I didn't make it in time for the #113 bus, not even in sight. The #1bus that followed wasn't crowded, so I got a seat. As I walked to the stop I marveled at the clearness of the early morning sky with the full moon of pale yellow hanging in plain view. I felt good, very little pain, a cloudless mind, no morning drowsiness. I felt blessed cause of you, my friends, and the freedom that I have experienced by what the Lord gives me to share. I am smiling. It is wonderful to share about our experiences with Heavenly Father. They are not always bright or chipper, just down to earth, honest. On the bus before we crossed over the bridge, I thought of the scripture where it says let my mouth speak of the testimony of the Lord **Psalm 145:21** "My mouth will speak in praise of the LORD. Let every creature praise his holy name for ever and ever."

Then Ps. 28 came to mind, this added to my much-loved blessing of the day.

I know you will be as blessed as I am today.

Matthew 10:29-31 "Are not two sparrows sold for a penny? Yet not one of them will fall to the ground apart from the will of your Father. 30And even the very hairs of your head are all numbered. 31So don't be afraid; you are worth more than many sparrows."

FOR THE BIRDS

The #1 bus was not crowded this morning so I took it rather then waiting for the #113, though about 4 stops after I got on there was standing room only. Within the first few blocks of the DT core there is an older school made of sandstone, which was converted to house some of the provincial parliament members offices, when they are in Calgary. There are always office workers in the building year-round. A typical sandstone structure made of huge blocks, a building material used in the early 1900', here in Calgary, it is still a nice-looking building. The grounds are well thought out and maintained, with a healthy stand of birches on the perimeter. During the early spring in the morning, I am amazed to see how many crows gather in their branches. Basically they become the leaves of the barren trees. I wonder, if there is a message here. Did you know that you don't call a group of crows a flock, they are known by a murder of crows? Why that word is used I don't know, nor do I know why they gather in that particular spot. But I think it is interesting that they would gather outside a building that houses politicians. Sorry just being a little mischievous. My thoughts went to another bird in the scriptures, the sparrow. In Matthew 10:29-31 Jesus talks about our worth and value in Him. The sparrows at that time were bought so they could be released as offerings, their value was minimal, almost worthless and of no concern to anyone due to their multitude in numbers. Heavenly Father knows when one falls to the ground even till this day. His awareness of all His creatures is phenomenal. His value of each living creature on this earth, no matter how many they number, is awesome.

Walking to work after I got off the bus, I passed a woman standing corner pillar of the store. She was talking about abortion being a crime. She had no sign, nothing, to indicate why she was there or with what organization. Just standing talking, not shouting, talking. At first, I was going to dismiss her as having a screw loose, then I thought what if she was a Christian and she thought this was the way to do things. I prayed for her instead, as I continued walking. In the next block sat a homeless man, he is in the same spot every morning lately, holding out a paper plate for people to put money in. Like the rest of the crowd I just pass him by, we think him insignificant. But even if we do, we serve a God who does not. So, what should we do, stop, talk to the lady by the pillar, or ask the man if he is hungry? I don't seem to have the time to do that in the mornings as I only have a few minutes between getting off my bus and arriving at work before I have to start. But I do not deem them worthless? My Christ stopped and spent time with people like them. He stopped His earthly life so I may have salvation and a way to commune with Him, Heavenly Father, Holy Spirit, our Trinity. I have no unction to do anything outside of to pray for them as I keep trucking along. If Father desires me to do something else then I will do it. I wonder if that is how the apostles were too? I have noticed that in scriptures they had passed by some of these folks too, not stopping till their attentions were drawn to do so.

"Father God, help me to view no one as being worthless or unvalued. Even in these days when we are judged by the way we look, speak, where we live, what we drive, so forth. Aid us in not thinking we are worthless because we have not achieved what others or ourselves think we should have achieved, or measured up to. Our worth and value lays with You Father and You see us as having great worth. Thank you, Jesus for paying that price. I am not worthy of that cost you paid, but You thought me worthy. That touches my soul in gratitude, humbleness, and thanksgivings. How can I measure up to that price? I can not do anything to achieve that, for You have taken care of that as well by providing Holy Spirit to guide us along the path of righteousness, to comfort us when we need it, to draw us closer to You, Father. Each intricate detail You thought out, You measured because You valued us so deeply. Your love for us is breathtaking Lord. Thank you.

Titus 2:15

"These, then, are the things you should teach. Encourage and rebuke with all authority. Do not let anyone despise you."

15 "These things speak, and exhort, and rebuke with all authority. Let no man despise thee."

I GIVE YOU AUTHORITY

As I was preparing for bed, I pondered about what Heavenly Father spoke about in Hebrews 5:11-21 this morning, regarding the elementary principle truths of God's word. I asked Him if He wanted to expand on that. His reply was quick, coming first in a form of a small vision. I feel, at this time, I am not to share this vision or it's meaning.

What is important to share is His question, "Do you know your authority?"

I understood that He was indicating this was one of the elementary principles we should know as believers in Christ.

What is our authority in Christ?

Being in various roles in ministry over the years I have experienced a few things. I have taken part in casting the enemy out of people. No, not the yelling and shouting type. Through being an observer I have found that a gentler but firmer style has an increased effectiveness than the other styles. In some of these sessions the spirit would question the authority of the person doing the deliverance. I have seen some doing the ministry get quite vibrantly verbal with the only result of the enemy ignoring them. The most prolific time was when the person responded... "you know whose authority." In this, there was no arrogance, only assurance of whom they served and what authority was extended to them. Our faith in what Christ has extended to us, the knowledge of what we have and how we are to use it.

The basic principle of authority in Christ comes from our relationship with Him, as the disciples had.

It is also knowing the type of authority as well as what authority means.

Authority, in the dictionary the meaning is, the power or right, the power to influence others, one's recognized knowledge about something.

The sociologist and philosopher Max Weber distinguishes three types of authority; charismatic, traditional, and legal-rational. Each of which corresponds to a brand of leadership that is operative in contemporary society. Traditional authority is the type that has been around longer, it is traditionally rooted in beliefs and the practices of society. Legal-rational authority requires a logical and systematic approach. In charismatic authority, confidence is the driving force with a person who has charisma. God has all these qualities, does He not?

It says in Titus to encourage and rebuke.

Encourage, how then is this authority?

The dictionary says encourage means; give support, confidence, or hope and advice to (someone) so that they will do or continue to do something, help, or stimulate (an activity, state, or view) to develop. In order to encourage someone effectively we must know firmly where the encouragement comes from. We, then, must know that the Lord has given us not only permission but authority in giving that encouragement. The authority of it is us knowing the character of Christ, Heavenly

7

Father and the Holy Spirit, the Holy Trinity. Being followers of this, He has confidence in us, extends authority under Him to step out to encourage people to follow Jesus, to come to Him personally, to know Him in a greater depth. Have you ever heard of anyone say, "Who gave you the right?" to say or do? Christ did.

Rebuke, many people take it upon their own views to tell someone else that they are doing something wrong. However, do they have the authority, in Christ to do so? This is a tricky one. One to ponder and pray about why the rebuke is giving. In many cases, it is authorized by Christ to straighten out an individual, a church, city or even a country, by the prophetic Christian people.

So, here it lays, God has given us authority, to comfort, encourage, uplift and correct. It is up to us to understand and exercise this authority under Jesus, aided by the Holy Spirit.

Luke 10:18-20 [18] He replied, "I saw Satan fall like lightning from heaven. [19] I have given you authority to trample on snakes and scorpions and to overcome all the power of the enemy; nothing will harm you. [20] However, do not rejoice that the spirits submit to you, but rejoice that your names are written in heaven."

Be blessed.

Max Weber - http://opinion.inquirer.net/85293/max-webers-3-types-of-authority

It's Autumn

Autumn is upon us Albertans, the burnt orange and bright yellow leaves mingle with the light green ones of summer, which are struggling to not change. It is a beautiful sight as one drives up the side of the hill on Sarcee Trial. Early Saturday evening as I headed towards a friend's, I looked over the city core. From that vantage point, luminous clouds were in the far distance, a pale rainbow displayed itself in front of them.

It made me think of God's promise not to cover the earth with water again. Reflecting reminded me of the promises He had made me based on His word. One in particular, He made many years ago, "I will never leave nor forsake you; you will always have a roof over your head, food and clothes on your back." No matter how difficult things have gotten from time to time over the years, He has been faithful to that promise to me. I thank Him many times for keeping it. That evening, I realized that His promises are one of His elementary principles of His Truth. I marveled how He is bringing forth the principles that I would have never thought about. Friday morning on the "late" #113 bus, yes, the early one was just a sound again this morning and the #1 bus did not have any seats available, Heavenly Father brought to mind Hebrews 9 to read. As I read it I saw more of His promises, some silent ones, others stated. I say silent because there is an implication of them, but not stated as actual promises.

One of the obvious ones is in verse 15, "the promised inheritance..." I know there is much more to this topic, hopefully Father will desire to expand on it one day soon. Yesterday, He drew my mind to share on a thought I had last Wednesday, on the way home from work. I usually catch the # 105 bus on the way home. Even though the #1 bus comes about the same time and it's stop is closer to my house. I chose the #105 bus, for it is less crowded, I don't mind the block and half walk to the house. Wednesday at work they had thrown a bridal shower for a lady recently married. I tried not to let it bother me but it did. On the way home I thought of my circumstance, of the "almost" wedding here in Calgary and the one to come. As I thought about it and struggled not to get depressed, Father likened my waiting for my earthly wedding to ours, as Christians. "His Bride" waiting to join Him. At first, I thought that was an interesting point but also thought it was rather morbid for we have to die first, but thought has no place in a blessing. It is a tangible promise that Leroy and I will be married soon. Even though it is not an on earth experience we will have with Christ, it is just as tangible a promise that we will be united with Christ, our Heavenly Bridegroom. This is a promise made by Father God. He has never broken His promises through His Word to us, nor in this present time. When He makes a personal promise to us, He also intends to keep them, especially this one. Praise God.

Bless you,

Exodus 34:14 – "Do not worship any other god, for the LORD, whose name is Jealous, is a jealous God."

Ecclesiastes 3:7- "a time to tear and a time to mend, a time to be silent and a time to speak…"

Jealousy of Time

The word jealous has bad connotations. In Galatians 5 it is listed as one of the acts of the sinful nature, yet in Exodus 34:14 God refers to himself as being a jealous God.

How then can we as believers in the True Word of God reconcile what He tells us in the Old & New Testaments?

Last night Leroy and I had a disagreement over our time together. Neither one of us handled it quite right. Upon pondering the disagreement this morning, on the bus, I missed the early #113, but this #1 was not crowded plus the driver was very friendly. During the ride I mussed about wanting a heart of forgiveness. being able to forgive as well as be forgiven with a pure heart. The Lord brought to mind how He is jealous. We humans can be multitasking people, it is preached to us from the pulpit of work ethics. It is revered if you shine forth as one in your resumes. There are times when multi-tasking is not appropriate. I recall when I use to spend hours just concentrating on God. I would make sure I had my cup of green tea and there was a long stretch when

I knew I wasn't going to be disturbed by anything or anyone. I would sit in silence with the scriptures, forcing my mind to focus in on one thing, Heavenly Father. I have noticed over the past couple of years this time has dissipated, other things have flooded into that time space that was only His. I must confess it has hindered my hearing from Him as acutely as I once could. Even my bus ride to work where I sat and contemplate upon Him, is not totally His time now. There are other people around me, my attention is easily diverted leading me to turn away from Him.

Is it an unreasonable request of our Heavenly Father to ask for total concentration on Him only? Was it an unreasonable request of Christ when He admonished the disciples about falling asleep as He prayed to His Father? Matthew 26:40 Then He returned to His disciples and found them sleeping. "Could you men not keep watch with me for one hour?" he asked Peter.

What is an hour to us? Could we not devote one entire unit of time to Him?

He is our Bridegroom, the Lover of our soul, the One we will spend eternity with.

Can you remember when you found your first love? How much time you wanted to spend with her/ him? How even a short period away from them was hard, then as time moved along, it wasn't as important to be with them so constantly. We call that period the getting to know one another when we desire to be immersed in their presence. This, right now on earth, is our courting time with Christ, even though it may span over years of our life. It is our time to come to know who He is. He does have one up on us though, He already knows who we are, better than we know ourselves. This period in earthly history is our time to get to know our Heavenly Lover, to come to recognize His voice, His presence, His breath upon us. I have fallen short of continuing with my part of the courtship with Him for I have divided it with an earthly loved one as well as family, friends, and life activities, including work.

"Heavenly Father, how our spirit longs to be with You, in the intimate silence of Your inner chamber. Yet our minds wander like that of the Jews long ago. We begin in our thoughts to concentrate after other things, other gods. Forgive us Father, for this, for we have stolen time away from You and away from ourselves where we could have spent it loving upon You as well as being loved upon by You. Thank you, Jesus, that You do not wane in this aspect of wooing us. You are a tired less Bridegroom, ever longing to purchase time from us so You can dote on us. Holy Spirit, I ask that today You would fall upon us and draw us, guide us, move us back into a mindset where we yearn after our quiet moments with Christ, let not our soul be satisfied until we do. Thank you Lord that you are faithful. For when we ask in Your Son's Name, You grant it. This I ask today in Jesus Christ's Name that You would grant us, my friends and I, this prayer of coming back into devoting time to You. Bless your Name, Lord. Amen.

Psalm 34:5 Those who look to him are radiant; their faces are never covered with shame.

MOUSE IN THE HOUSE

When I first started sharing my bus ride thoughts each day, I sort of wondered to Heavenly Father why? There were moments where I was stressed out about it. What if I don't get anything? Yes, I am chuckling at myself. Then I settled down and said, "Father thank you for your blessing, if you have something every day or not, you have blessed me."

I sometimes wonder with all the profound things God gives me, and with me nattering, why He doesn't say "Maggie, take a pill." He doesn't, He just lovingly listens, then responds, most of the time in a loving way. It is always loving even if it is a flick on the ear. Today I inquired about what He would like to share. He brought my attention around to my visitor in the wee hours of the morning. Yes, there is a mouse in the house. It is fall, they are looking for housing too. I thought about why we don't like these little critters in our homes. We seldom see them, except me, they seem to like to show themselves to me.

When I was living at my daughters my room was in the basement. Sewing one night, I saw one quickly climb over a picture, honest, it steadied itself to show me it's butt. MMM – cheeky mouse. Well, we set a trap the next day and that was it for him. We, humans, don't like rodents because they are filthy, get into our food and other things.

On the late #113 bus this morning I thought about what mouse I had in my house, meaning inside me, was there something that has crept in and is nibbling away at something precious? As we rode along the river, I marveled at the early morning blue sky being highlighted by the bright yellowed leaves of autumn, Heavenly Father said, "Like every city, there are mice that creep into it as well." I thought that was interesting, we don't see them, but they are infectious. They begin to chew away at the structure of our society. There are even mice in the churches. Ones who go with no intention of serving God, yet they sit in the pews and nibble away at the foundations of what our churches stand for. I could go on in more detail about these three topics, but I don't want to use this daily sharing for any platform. What I do sense is Heavenly Father challenging us today about seeking Him to show us any mice either in our own lives, in our city or even in our congregations.

"Show us Father, first how to deal effectively with vermin. Then reveal them to us, Lord, the ones we need to be gentle with and ones we need to be forceful with. I do understand Father that they are to be removed so they do not cause any more destruction. Thank you, Father, for your challenge to us, your every present desire to clean us up and draw us closer to you. Thank you, for your Word today, Lord. If we do look to You, then we have nothing to be ashamed of, for it is Your working on our lives that removes that shame. Thank you, Lord."

John 9 :3 "Neither this man nor his parents sinned," said Jesus, "but this happened so that the work of God might be displayed in his life. 4As long as it is day, we must do the work of him who sent me. Night is coming, when no one can work. 5While I am in the world, I am the light of the world."

Malachi 3 :3 He will sit as a refiner and purifier of silver; he will purify the Levites and refine them like gold and silver. Then the LORD will have men who will bring offerings in righteousness, **4** and the offerings of Judah and Jerusalem will be acceptable to the LORD, as in days gone by, as in former years.

Malachi 4: 3 Then you will trample down the wicked; they will be ashes under the soles of your feet on the day when I do these things," says the LORD Almighty. 4 "Remember the law of my servant Moses, the decrees and laws I gave him at Horeb for all Israel.

NO BASIS FOR CHARGE

The day started a little earlier then usual, I had to take my car into the shop. This garage is about 10 mins west of me but on the same route as the #105 and #1 buses. I caught the #1. I see now, why it is so crowded when it hits my stop, it is already half full where I caught it today. It was harder to focus with so many people talking and just being present. But I did try. Yesterday was a difficult day for me, hearing another friend getting married and me just sitting here waiting. The thoughts, came in with the could "haves" or should "bes". When I got home last night, I had a good cry, a little snooze, then I was better. Now this morning I am eager to see what Father has to share. I didn't really understand the scriptures at first, that He had given me. I read them, then sat back asking for Holy Spirit to move, to reveal till I could finally see it. I was moved.

"...no basis for a charge against this man." Lk 3:4.

No matter how hard we look at the ground, saying "Lord, you have done nothing for me, whoa is me, you treat me unfairly, you don't care."

There is no basis for that charge against Christ. He extended His love to us in salvation and continues to do so, especially during the worse times, if we chose to see it.

Then there is the question, Why? Why me? Why this?

"...that the work of God might be displayed in his life." John 9: 3

Do we really understand the ramification of that statement? Our natural knee jerk reaction when something bad happens is to blame. Blame ourselves, first usually, "oh I must have sinned, I am not good enough, I failed." Many times, it is none of these. Though we can not hide behind that reason either. Let's look at it this way. I feel God trusts us enough to allow us to experience hardship, believing that we will dig deep and press into Him, resulting in us allowing Him to show forth His work. There are various reasons why I am still sitting here in Calgary, many if we wish to blame this or that or who. Or could it be for another reason?

On my way back home from the Vancouver border, after being turned away from going to the states, God said, "what if I was sending you back for your son? What would you say?" Now this is in reply to hours of me ragging on Him. I had to think about it for a few seconds. Cheeky as I am, and wishing many times I wasn't, my response was, "This better be darn good." Has this going back for my son amounted to anything in this area, not yet. When both Leroy and I got back to our separate homes, he said, "God has you there for a reason." I have had to submit to that, for a couple of times people have said to me, separately, that God brought me back for them.

John 9:4...." we must do the work of him who sent me. Night is coming,"

I have work to do here, still, it is to share what has happened to me over the past year and how I have emerged from, it is a witness of God's work in my life. What you have gone through, going through or how you will be during this time as well as after, is a witness of God's work in you. Step back, ask Holy Spirit to reveal it to you.

What an honour. What a privilege for Father in Heaven to say, "I chose you, to go through this so I may use you." Wow Hey!

He is refining us. He is purifying us. That we will bring offerings in righteousness, acceptable to Him. Malachi 3:3. Did you know He is proud of you? He is. Even of me, with my cheekiness, hissy fits and pouting. He has dotingly loved upon me. This is so I can be all that He has created me to be. The same is with you, you are no different. Remember the day I spoke about promises? After all His work on us He gives us another promise here. All this refining, all this purifying so that you, my friend, can trample the enemy to ashes under your feet. What a rush! My, my, my, I want to do a trampling dance. Lord let your day come so we can do this trampling dance on our enemy.

Malachi 4:4 "Remember the law of my servant Moses, the decrees and laws I gave him at Horeb for all Israel."

Base your life on these allowing the Lord to expand them with His work in His grace and mercy extended to us in the New Testament.

There is no basis for a charge against Him nor the wondrous work He does in our lives.

Bless you Father, thank you. Amen.

PREPARING FOR THE WEATHER

If you are familiar with Calgary then you know that our weather changes can be dramatic and sudden. Not like the storms one would expect in their season. Last week we were enjoying sunny blue skies with temperatures in the high 20's – mid 30's oC (mid 70's – high 80's oF). Tonight, it will be about 5oC (low 40's oF) with a mixture of rain & snow.

Yesterday, I was extremely exhausted, due to being woken up early in the morning from a nightmare. I felt I didn't hear very well from the Lord, even though He did give me a scripture during the bus ride,

Jeremiah 10: 15 "They are worthless, the objects of mockery; when their judgment comes, they will perish."

I didn't really understand it. When I was on the first contract at a small oil company, one of the ladies came into the well file room and announced she was a Wiccan witch. It did go with the conversation my co-worker and I were having. Yesterday, this lady and I met again in someone else's office to go over some work. I felt a spiritual battle begin to rage inside, one for dominancy. Because I am sensitive to feeling spiritual activity, I find it is a waste of time to fight it. I simply said in my mind, "The Living God of Israel, Yahweh reigns over all.", then quoted Jeremiah 10:15. That ended the battle.

This morning coming to work I asked for another scripture, and I read Romans 12:5 "So in Christ we who are many form one body, and each member belongs to all the others."

I see Heavenly Father is making a parallel between our preparing ourselves, physically and, mentally for the coming weather changes.

How is it then we are not preparing for the battle that can come at any time with any force by any means?

Are we prepared mentally, for confrontations with someone who so blatantly serves the other side?

Are we prepared in strength and stature mentally, so the enemy will not take us down?

The onslaught is on and it will become more ferocious. I wish I could say other, but it is reality, we face the time of season where anything can happen.

Are we prepared?

A topic a person could go further on, but Heavenly Father desires me to end here. Perhaps it is just enough to quiz ourselves about… "Am

I prepared?" "What weather is ahead of me?" I believe Heavenly Father will not let anything come upon us without some warning, no matter how subtle it is.

Are our eyes open to see it, our ears open to hear, our minds open to comprehend?

"I bless you, my dear friends, in the name of our Lord Jesus Christ, with those open eyes and ears and minds, so you will not be caught unawares or unguarded. I ask, Lord, that You move all of us to get and be prepared for the weather. Amen.

God Bless

Ezekiel 20
Rebellious Israel vs. 1-29
Judgment and Restoration vs. 30 – 44
Verse 42 "Then you will know that I am the LORD, when I bring you into the land of Israel, the land I had sworn with uplifted hand to give to your fathers."

Sharing History

It was a chilling morning today. Warnings not to travel west of the city due to fresh snow on the roads, especially closer to and in the mountain area. Yes, the Alberta fall is in full swing, though we can still get some pretty mild weather.

As I rode the bus into the downtown core, I saw in one of the smaller restaurants a wall mural.

This reminded me of a restaurant my parents had taken me to when I was a child. I can only remember the towering walls, they may not have been that high but I was a kid. On this vast mural was cowboys and their ranching life. I then thought when my Dad passes away, he is the only one that will know where that restaurant was located. My dad knows a lot of history about Calgary, he shares only when asked. My thoughts were all over the place and rolling in, for the next one was regarding a denomination that I had studied when I was involved with a group doing research on revivals. I went to see the pastor of the denomination, I was assigned to study. I found out about its history, even though his family line with it was from the start he knew very little about the denomination's past. In fact, he had just done research on it when I met him. I was baffled as to why he did not know of the richness of their faith and prayers that brought about this denomination. At that time, Heavenly Father, brought to mind, how many, including the Israelites, did not and do not pass down their spiritual history of God's moving.

It saddens me.

My maternal grandmother's father was an elder in their church, experiencing many miracles, but the only time she had spoken of it was after I had become a Christian and taking her occasionally to church with me.

Visiting my paternal grandfather in Kelowna one year, I inquired about his mom who was a Native Canadian. It took him a little time to share that she was very involved with the Anglican Church, she would visit many people when they were ill, bringing them food.

I realized after he had shared that I did have a rich Christian history in my background, but few had shared it with their family or carried it further.

This morning I quizzed myself, what am I doing to share with my grandsons about my walk with Christ? I used to take my oldest grandson to church with me till he didn't want to go any more. My younger grandkids go regularly with their mom. But what have I done to give them a piece of my Christian history? Sounds like I have a project coming up to write some kind of story or diary for them.

"Lord, I ask today that in each one of us You will not let our history of walking with You, Jesus, die with us. But from our lips we will share about our trials, tribulations and how Your mercy, grace and love brought us through. That You will inspire us to share verbally and in written form our relationship with You, Lord. Let not our children or our children's children grow up not knowing about You, knowing their rich Christian background. Thank you, Father that You reached down to us through the ages and brought us to know You. Bless us today, Lord." Amen.

Jeremiah 10: 20 My tent is destroyed; all its ropes are snapped. My sons are gone from me and are no more; no one is left now to pitch my tent or to set up my shelter.

TENT PEGS AND TERRITORIES

Calgary was covered in fog this morning.

As the late #113 bus emerged from underneath the 16th avenue over pass, heading east on Memorial drive, one could see cyclists making their way towards downtown on the popular pathway that skirts the river. Even though, they were beginning to be shrouded in the fog with only their blinking red tail lights showing that someone was there.

I relish mornings like these. Some would say I am crazy because of the fine mist that washes over you, but to me it is a refreshing quality.

As the bus trundled along I was still grappling with a conversation that I had with a brother in Christ last night. I know it was not him who rattled me but that which he has allowed to come upon him. I pray desperately that he will soon emerge from its grasp and be the free, wholesome man God has created him to be. But I was still puzzled at why I would still be agitated.

In the early portion of my walk with Christ, He referred to me as like a puppy who grabs hold of a wet cloth, no matter how hard you shake it, the little thing doesn't let go. My daughter expressed that's how she feels she is like also. I guess like daughter like mother. Oh, dear are we ready for that yet, two of us...chuckle.

The scripture that came to mind today was Jeremiah 10:20. This puzzled me even more as its relationship to my friend, so I put it aside, occasionally enquiring the Lord about it while I worked. I thought about the prayer of Jabez. Odd huh, I could not see how the two, the scripture and Jabez, could match. I wondered why, for Jabez spoke of increase and Jeremiah the tent being destroyed. You most likely have thought what the connection is, by now. It is the focus. Jabez's prayer is very simple.

1 Chronicles 4:10 Jabez cried out to the God of Israel, "Oh, that you would bless me and enlarge my territory! Let your hand be with me, and keep me from harm so that I will be free from pain." And God granted his request.

What was the difference between Jabez and all of Jerusalem?

The answer is in the verse before ten, "9 Jabez was more honorable…."

Now is this to say if you don't have answered prayers you are not honourable… No. What I feel the Lord would like to express today is "What is your focus when you come to Me and pray? Where is your heart, what is it that you really want? Your will or Mine?

We can kid ourselves, that what we want is justified and follows His good, when really it is our own desires which wants the upper hand. My hand is up, been there, done that and have been shown it. "Thank you Lord for showing me."

"Lord enlarge my territory, but not mine Lord, yours in me, so that I will seek after that which you desire me to. When I ask "enlarge my territory Lord, let it be, enlarge the area where I will be most effective for You. Enlarge my area of thought so I may dwell specifically on You and Your ways, not mine. Lord I ask for a favour today, those areas which my friends desire to have their territories enlarged in, let You be the center of it, so they may see what portion is theirs and which portion is Yours. Then Lord bless them with the abilities to adjust their perspectives so they will also be most honourable before You."

Jeremiah spoke the ending prayer most appropriately in Jeremiah 10: 23 - 24 "I know, O LORD, that a man's life is not his own; it is not for man to direct his steps. Correct me, LORD, but only with justice— not in your anger, lest you reduce me to nothing."

I add, "but raise us up out of the dust Father so that we may serve You, how you have created us to do. Bless us Lord with the enlargement of You inside of us, Your presence about us, our knowledge of whom You are. Thank you, Father, for all blessings flow from You." Amen.

Matthew 5:2-5 "and he began to teach them saying: 3 Blessed are the poor in spirit, for theirs is the kingdom of heaven. 4 Blessed are those who mourn, for they will be comforted. 5 Blessed are the meek, for they will inherit the earth."

THE MIST ROSE

The mist rose off the Bow River this morning, like smoke from a campfire, it curled its way amongst the golden leaved trees, on the embankment. Pink hued clouds streaked across the azure blue morning sky, as white winged gulls swooped down to land on the bare river rocks. We are now officially in the first week of fall.

I wished I had ear plugs this morning so the tinny sound exuding from someone's headphones wouldn't intrude my thoughts, but wishing more, that I hadn't removed the zipper from my fall jacket. Before leaving, I wiped it on the purple jacket, forgetting it was in midst of repair. I realized that point when I was half way down the alley. It was too late to turn back, but it held closed, sufficiently.

I prayed for a scripture on the way downtown, Matthew 5:2-5 came to mind. Looking up the meaning of the word poor, at work, because I wanted to get a wider scope of the meaning. One particular word loomed out at me and took me back to an elevator ride I took.

Poor (humble, insignificant, lowly, modest, unpretentious)

Pretentious, Father called me that once after I had a little hissy fit about something.

I lived at an apartment at that time, leaving it to get my mail on the main floor, I stepped into the elevator. The Lord spoke quite clearly saying, "you are pretentious, aren't you?" At that moment, I wasn't sure what pretentious meant, though something inside told me it wasn't good. I don't remember what I had the hissy fit about, but it was around the time I didn't want anything to do with the prophetic or prophetic people. Annoyed at other prophetic people, pastors, and generally just people. He probably told me to give some kind of prophetic word and I didn't want to. Sort of makes you wonder how I have survived this long without God zapping me. Though times like that I have seen how deep His love, patience and tolerance is of us, "humanoids." Those are times of humbling, character building or smashing which every comes first. When I got back into my apartment I looked up the word in my dictionary, and yes, repented profusely for my attitude. Some of His most profound and awesome prophetic words have come to me when my face is in the floor. As is His way, He also drew me away from the negativism of the word to see that one little sentence of positive. An aspiration or intention that may or may not reach fulfillment.

An aspiration or intention. I think that is what I felt this morning too, when I read the scripture. I have been bothered by the fact that some of my friends are going through hard times right now and I don't have anything to say to soothe them, some are in pain, I don't have healing hands to relieve that for them. Blessed are the poor, blessed are those that mourn, blessed are those who are meek.

"Father you know those friends of mine that are troubled, who are in turmoil, that suffer pain. Ones who are bewildered by situations that come upon them over and over again, even through their trying to do things right for You. Lord I ask this day that those who receive this will be blessed for their humbleness of spirit.

Father if there still needs to be more humbleness then I ask you, let them know before and during the process of them gaining it.

Lord there are some of my friends here that are mourning for various different things and in different ways, comfort them Father, Holy Spirit comfort them, please.

There are some who are trying to balance out that meekness, how to be assertive when it is needed as not to be walked all over. How to be Your kind of meek Jesus. For there is strength and stability in Your kind of meekness Lord.

Bless us Lord for we are frail. We do tend to flop around like fish out of water. But with all that flopping, we do try desperately to be for You, Christ. For our love for you is deep and wanting. Have mercy upon us & bless us with your love patience & tolerance. Thank you Father" Amen

John 10:4 "When he has brought out all his own, he goes on ahead of them, and his sheep follow him because they know his voice. **16** I have other sheep that are not of this sheep pen. I must bring them also. They too will listen to my voice, and there shall be one flock and one shepherd. **27** My sheep listen to my voice; I know them, and they follow me."

The Voice

Through the years many have asked me, "how do you know you're hearing God's voice and not your own or someone else's?"

I am not special in how I hear or know that I hear God's voice speaking to me. We all have had an experience of Him speaking to us, more than once. Before you came to know Jesus Christ as your personal Saviour, you heard God's voice speaking to your heart. As you have asked direction from time to time you have heard God's voice. To the why I hear as I do, I cannot totally say the why. I have spent years testing, to make sure that it was His voice, I have never stopped that testing. The depth of my gifting demands it. I have spent hours on my face or just sitting, listening. Always given a choice to if I want to do this or not. Taking the above scriptures literally, my desire was to recognize His voice when He calls, speaks, or sings. Did you know Heavenly Father sings over you? He does.

You may be asking me right now, what tests that I use, or have used to know it was or is Christ speaking to me. One is the scriptures. At the beginning, I would ask Him to speak through the scriptures to me, verifying that was Him. He did. But that is not full proof for the enemy also knows God's word, as we see in his attempt to dissuade Christ. But how is the scripture used? Is it to benefit only ourselves? Or is it used to Glorify our Creator and minister to others?

Secondly, I bounced off others what I had heard, asking them to inquire of the Lord if I was truly hearing correctly. Not just those friends who would say yes, but those I knew who would correct me.

Thirdly, bring it back. Sounds odd eh! But that is one of the tests I use, "Lord if this is of you then you bring it back to my mind when you desire." Surprisingly sometimes the thought I had, never returned. The words I had heard did return to my mind the following day, I would continue to quiz asking for insight.

Many have said if you can't find what He says to you in the scriptures then it is not Him. I have found that is not the case, there are many times He says things that I can't find in the scriptures, that is why I employed other means to test whether, or not, it is His voice. For instance, when I shared about Him calling me pretentious, can you find that in the scriptures? No, but was it God's voice? Yes, because He did it to make me stop, submit to correction and incorporate that correction into my life. It served a purpose; His glory was shown forth in the molding of me to be humble and a effective in my ministry to His children.

Why am I sharing about this today? To encourage you to take moments in the day to ask Heavenly Father to speak to you clearly. Write these down, test them. It is His voice that we should recognize when the enemy's comes, when the world comes, when our own self crowds in on us. We need to hear His voice to calm us, strengthen us, to encourage us. We are His sheep, it is His voice we should recognize above all others. Like a child knows their mother's or father's voice.

Psalm 34:4 "I prayed to the Lord and He answered me, freeing me from all my fears."

Be blessed today for you are His blessed child.

Hebrews 5:11-21

"11 We have much to say about this, but it is hard to explain because you are slow to learn. 12 In fact, though by this time you ought to be teachers, you need someone to teach you the elementary truths of God's word all over again. You need milk, not solid food! 13 Anyone who lives on milk, being still an infant, is not acquainted with the teaching about righteousness. 14 But solid food is for the mature, who by constant use have trained themselves to distinguish good from evil."

WARNING AGAINST FALLING AWAY

The early #113 was more than elusive today, it was out of sight. As I walked across the patio to get to the back steps I heard the bus. I knew which one it was. Only five minutes though for a #1 bus came with empty seats on it. I felt tense this morning which made it difficult to concentrate on anything. But as I pushed my mind into saying, "I praise you Lord" repeatedly, relaxation came.

Hebrews 5:12 came to mind and once more I was eager to get to work to read it. When I could, I felt I was supposed to read from verse 11-14. The title they had given it was Warning Against Falling Away from God. When I worked at a large oil company in the 1970's to 1990's, a group of Christians had a noon hour Bible study. One year we decided that we were going to do a study called Back to the Basics. Determining in ourselves to remain open, we were all coined "mature" Christians but of different denominations. Each one of the regulars studied a certain topic then presented it in a Bible Study format. What amazed us the most was there were areas in each one of us where we were weak in knowledge of the topic we studied. Generally speaking, this weakness affects the foundation of our walk with Christ.

In this portion of scripture, the speaker is reprimanding the listener for just that. "12 In fact, though by this time you ought to be teachers, you need someone to teach you the elementary truths of God's word all over again…"

What are the elementary truths of God's Word? For instance, do we know all the different types of baptisms explained in the scriptures, knowing what their purposes are for? Am I assured of my salvation in Christ and why? Can I, if called upon, teach the elementary principle truths of God's word to a none or a new believer?

Verse 13 "Anyone who lives on milk, being still an infant, is not acquainted with the teaching about righteousness."

I sometimes wonder if we as Christians require refresher courses on the basics. We are so busy running to that meeting or this conference on various other topics, but in doing so have we kept up our knowledge of the basics. I know for myself, if someone came up to me today, asking me to lead them to Christ, I would have to hesitate on what exactly to say to them. Oh, I do know the sinner's prayer having prayed it with non-believers but what would I teach them to begin with. Do you remember your first Bible lesson on becoming a believer?

Verse "14 But solid food is for the mature, who by constant use have trained themselves to distinguish good from evil."

The enemy is so hotly in pursuit of us. We need to be at the point where we are on solid food so that we can distinguish between good and evil. I have seen too many Christians during my walk with Him, that have fallen due to some very simplistic weakness. It leaves me in a bit of a daze, "how can they Lord?" Having a prophetic gifting, He has shown me sometimes why people have fallen. What they have to do to stand up again to continue on. I not only encourage this to the person, but I also apply it to my life. I am all too aware of the four fingers are pointing back at me.

"Lord, You know the weak areas in our foundations. I ask for all my friends and myself that You would reveal those weak areas to us. Then guide us, Holy Spirit, to how we can go about shoring those foundations up by reacquainting ourselves with the elementary principles of Your Word. Strengthen us Father, so we may distinguish between good & evil and are acquainted with righteousness. Thank you, Father. Amen

1 Corinthians 3:16 "Don't you know that you yourselves are God's temple and that God's Spirit lives in you?"

WHICH BUS WOULD YOU TAKE?

Today could be a Monday. In a sense it is, for it is a Tuesday after a long weekend and things have started off like a Monday for me.

I almost caught the early #113 bus, however narrowly missed it once more for I had to waste a few extra steps to put out the garbage.

A #1 bus came along about 5 mins after. Opting to wait, for there was standing room only, I realized that I should have worn a light jacket instead of not wearing one at all. Even though the forecasters predicted a high of 26 C (about 84 F) for the day, the temperature in the morning was 12 C (about 56 F) when I left. Evidentially, I had neglected to factor in the wind, which was a bit chilly. Upon enquiring of the Lord for a scripture before leaving the house, 1 Cor. 3:16 came to mind. While on the bus I struggled with negative thoughts about other people as well as myself. Before I looked up the scripture I checked for my reading glasses, there was a wrong pair in my prescription eye glass case. They were drug store ones, a bit stronger than what I need. What can I say? It is, after all, a Monday / Tuesday. When I finally look up the scripture, it brought me back to my thoughts while commuting. I am not bound by a church or denomination where they say I should think this or that way. I house the Holy Spirit; therefore, my thoughts should be subjected to the Spirit of God. Difficult task. It is much easier to be dictated to by some outside structural component then to acquiesce ourselves to an abstract force. Yet in true reality the latter is more tangible than the former, for God is omni-present, the former is not. With the churches or denominations, we are left on our own when outside its walls finding it easier to hide or set up a false presentation. The Holy God of Israel, Yahweh is always with us, in our movements, our inner thoughts which we hide from others. We are not left on our own as Christ daily, hourly – every second walks beside us. His voice constantly whispers in our ears, if we chose to hear it. More often than not, we are busy seeking a more conspicuous voice, while He chooses a quieter, more subtle way. I am God's temple, God's Spirit lives in me, so that verse says, therefore as I surrender to that concept, I must readily and continually repent for allowing the invasion of negativism into my life, whether it be from the enemy or myself. If I do not repent then I risk losing the ability in living in harmony with other believers.

Please, understand, I do recommend fellowshipping with other believers in a church setting. It is health and scriptural. Few can stand firm spiritually outside it walls. A church should offer acceptance, protection, this is the ideal but not always the fact.

There are times when Heavenly Father will tell us there is something wrong with a person or situation this we should heed Him. I am speaking more of acknowledging that the Holy Spirit does dwell in us when we become believers in the Living God, Elohim. It is part of Christ's promise when He left this earth. It is easy to forget this principle as we function in a world of sight and physically tangible things.

My question to myself today is, what am I doing to house Holy Spirit? Have I crowded Him out of one area to resign Him to another specific one where He is to "stay put"?

"Holy Spirit, you are a strange concept to us much of the time. We understand You, Heavenly Father and your Son Jesus Christ, but when it comes to Holy Spirit dwelling in us, we are confused. Lord, I ask today that You enable us to understand. In our own might we cannot do this. It takes a relationship with you Jesus, so our mindset will un-crowd itself, to accommodate this space for Holy Spirit's dwelling. Amen"

Bless you,

Psalm 119:23-29 - 24 Your laws please me, they give me wise advice. 25 I lie in the dust, revive me by your word. 26 I told you my plans, and you answered. Now teach me your decrees. 27 Help me understand the meaning of your commandments, and I will meditate on your wonderful deeds. 28 I weep with sorrow, encourage me by your word. 29 Keep me from lying to myself, give me the privilege of knowing your instructions.

A Privilege & Honour

I got up late today and drove to work. If I had waited for the bus I would have been a half hour late thus not being able to leave work till 4:30 pm instead of 4 pm. I have a problem with crowds so I chosen to get up early in order to leave early. Unfortunately, it doesn't always work that way. By driving gives me the option to get to work at 7:15am. So, I had even more time to type up this story before I started work at 7:30am.

The drive was in the dark, there was a light fog in my area as I approached the down town core. I could see the dark outlines of the barren trees against the back drop of the city lights. A fall morning, though today wasn't as chilly as the past three days had been. Leaving my car in the parkade, I began the two-block walk to my office, I noticed that I was kind of going against the flow of the crowd. Everyone seemed to be coming towards me with no one really wanting to step aside to let me through. There was a line up for Timmy's aka Tim Horton's, a very popular Canadian coffee shop, the last person must have had to wait at least 10 mins to get their coffee, plus there were still people lining up after them.

I pondered about the going against the flow bit. I felt that as Christians we basically all do it from one degree to another. What makes us go against the flow though? What makes us different outside of just believing that Christ lives? Reading the scripture today, I saw some of what makes us different. We seek Him, His ways, while others do not. The news reported that in one village in India wanted to cut down a dead tree, but the farmer whose land it was on said it spoke to him, as a result the village began to worship this dead tree. We read a scripture a few days ago that spoke about that, worshipping dead things. What makes us, Christians, different and go against the flow is we worship a Living God. In the Psalms verses above, we see the help we derive from is His Word? His laws give us wise advice, "Thou shalt not kill". I think that is wise, for if we did we would get jail time. However just not jail time, we would get mental torment for we stepped out of our boundaries and took another living beings life. Someone God created. "I lie in the dust, revive me by your word." When we are down, depressed, Him speaking to us through His Word, can revitalize, resuscitate, and bring us back to life. Even though we think at times He does not answer us. He does, subtle ways, sometimes outspoken ways, but He does not ignore us. I like the last verse, in this Psalm, the best. "Keep me from lying to myself." How many times have we talked ourselves in to justifying what we have done, even when we know that it is wrong? I have always felt that my mind sometimes wants to rule my spirit and my heart sometimes wants to be the boss. But, it is only through seeking Him which quiets the mind and soul. I can see the Truth, He gives me the privilege of knowing His instructions. Have you ever thought of knowing Him, knowing His instructions, as a privilege? I looked this word up, here are a few of it's meanings, freedom, opportunity, advantage, honour, pleasure, joy, favor, benefit. Just to know that Heavenly Father shows partiality towards us, wow, eh. Think about each one of the words in the description of privilege.

"Thank you, Heavenly Father, that you show partiality and favour towards us, Your children. In giving us the freedom, opportunity and advantage to know the honour, the benefit it is to serve You with pleasure and joy. Blessed be Your Name, oh, Lord God on High."

Philemon 1: 7 "Your love has given me great joy and encouragement, because you, brother, have refreshed the hearts of the saints." Verse 25 "The grace of the Lord Jesus Christ be with your spirit."

A USEFUL PURPOSE

Am I on a roll now? I caught the early #113 again, this morning. Sounds funny to make that kind of a feat, but we all have things in our lives that seem small to others yet it is an accomplishment to us for various reasons.

It is Girl Guide cookie time once more. How do I know that? A lady got on the bus with a box of cookies and before you know it she had sold 4 boxes to people, without trying. No, I didn't buy a box, although tempted. I figured it would too much of a hassle to rummage in my backpack for my wallet, it would be easier to wait for those moms at work to mention something. It was nice to see, though, this kind of a community spirit on a bus. With smiles and chuckles as some discussed how fast they would be devoured.

As I prepared for bed last night, the Lord gave me Philemon to read. This morning, I pondered it as I rode on the bus. I asked what message was in it, His reply was, "what is the essence of it?" In Philemon, Paul is writing to fellow believers while he and Timothy are in jail. He writes for them to accept Onesimus. I like how he put it in verse 11 "Formerly he was useless to you, but now he has become useful both to you and to me." Basically, that was us, before we determined in our hearts to be His workers with our focus on Him and Him alone. Formerly, we were useless to Father God as workers. We had no desire to pray, no desire to speak about Him or His word of Life. Yet, as we grew in knowledge, we became useful to Christ in advancing His Kingdom. There may be moments still where we feel useless, thinking we don't do much. I assure you, if you seek Heavenly Father, desiring for Holy Spirit to fill you and aid you in the task Christ has set before you, you are doing something. Yes, your mind may seem to be in a fog from time to time, your life too busy to even think a thought, but where is your heart. If it is for Christ, to be used of Him, then you are useful. He is either preparing you to be used or He has you doing His work now.

Ask Him today, "Jesus, what stage am I in, being prepared or ready to do your work? Show me Lord what I can do for you today? Can I smile at someone or in that show them your heart for them? What can I do – for you – Lord today?

I want to repeat Paul's words over as a prayer from my heart to you, verses 5,6 and 25 "because I hear about your faith in the Lord Jesus and your love for all the saints. I pray that you may be active in sharing your faith, so that you will have a full understanding of every good thing we have in Christ. The grace of the Lord Jesus Christ be with your spirit. Thank you, Father, for my friends."

God Bless your day today.

Romans 10:15 "And how can they preach unless they are sent? As it is written, "How beautiful are the feet of those who bring good news!" "7 How beautiful on the mountains are the feet of the messenger who brings good news, the good news of peace and salvation, the news that the God of Israel reigns!"

BEAUTIFUL SENT ONES

It was a difficult morning today. Even though my emotions were fluctuating for no reason, it makes it a struggle to concentrate. I was able to get my thoughts under control and pursued Heavenly Father in what He would like to share today. First reading Romans 10:15, then Is. 52:7.

Did you know your feet are beautiful?

They are not only "...shod with the preparation of the gospel of peace;" Ephesians 6:15, but they are also beautiful. We bring with us the gospel of Christ. Our mountain is Christ Himself, He is our foundation, through Him we share with the world Him and what He embodies. We bring "good news", peace, among war, fighting and turmoil. We do not have to be in Iraq or where ever they are having another war. We can be here right in the middle of where we live to be in the middle of turmoil. It is all around us. Just listen to the ones you associate with. Don't their lives reflect turmoil? Yet, in this we bring the good news of peace, peace in Christ. The good news of salvation, salvation in Christ. For from the grasp of the enemy's lair we bring the good news of salvation of Christ. Among those who worship "dead" things we bring the good news of a Living God, one who reigns now and forever more. No matter what we or they are going through right at the moment, we have been prepared by Him to be messengers of the gospel of Christ. We have been sent - Luke 4: 18 "The Spirit of the Lord is on me, because he has anointed me to preach good news to the poor. He has sent me to proclaim freedom for the prisoners and recovery of sight for the blind, to release the oppressed, 19 to proclaim the year of the Lord's favor."

"How wonderful, what a privilege. He has chosen you, chosen you from the womb to go through what you have gone through and what you are going through, so He may send you out.

You are a beautifully sent one. You may say, "I can't say this or that to people regarding Christ or who am I going to say it too?" Stop saying that, now. Look at yourself in the mirror, say – "I am a beautifully sent one. God has chosen me to send out with His good news. Thank you, Lord. Lord, You have given me the opportunity to share Your good news with whom You desire me to, today."

This should be our main focus. It is not what shall I wear today, or where shall I go on holidays. Yes, those decisions are in our lives, but our main focus as followers of Christ should be doing what He has sent us out among the world to do. "Oh, I can't evangelize, I'm not equipped." Do you know why Christ died for you? Do you know why you turned to Him for your salvation? If you know the answers to those questions then you are equipped. You are a beautifully sent one. Even there where you are sitting feeling useless and depressed, you are still a beautifully sent one. For He is using this moment to draw you closer to Him in your troubles, to seek Him. He is preparing you. He sees your potential as one of His beautifully sent ones. He has put a call on your life.

Bless you my dear friend, beautifully sent one.

Matthew 25:2-5 "Five of them were foolish and five were wise. 3The foolish ones took their lamps but did not take any oil with them. 4The wise, however, took oil in jars along with their lamps. 5 The bridegroom was a long time in coming, and they all became drowsy and fell asleep."

FUTURE OF THE PAST

Small things in life can make people happy. I was up in time to just catch the early #113 bus. I made it to the lights before he did, pushing the button to cross, so I waved him down as he started to pass. He stopped and waited for me to trundle along. He was a pleasant person, I thanked him when I got on. A relatively empty bus it became crowded by the time we got down to the river area. I sat on the other side so I didn't get to see the river this morning but I still prayed as we moved along.

Yesterday my infected tooth had a flare up so I was at home nursing that unable to really concentrate on the Lord, when I should have. Though in the evening, He began speaking about the "past of the future".

This morning I asked for a scripture to support what He was saying. If you think I know my Bible well you are wrong, I don't, that is why I ask Heavenly Father for scriptures, then read to see what His Word says. I can remember excerpts of what The Word says but I don't remember where they are. I wondered what this scripture, Matthew 25:2-5, had to do with what He had begun saying regarding the "past of the future".

I find it interesting that Jesus made a point to say the foolish ones, then the wise ones, for we know they represent the unprepared and the prepared. But, He went on to say they all became drowsy and fell asleep. Both the unprepared and the prepared fell asleep while waiting.

So, what makes us drowsy in our waiting for our Bridegroom?

One is the heaviness of our past. If, left unattended to, it can become toxic as issues grow stale and mutate. Our past in Christ should become a witnessing tool only of how His mercy, grace and love has worked in our lives. To make it that way, we must go back hand in hand with Christ, asking Him to examine each step, inquiring of Him to show us what we have left unattended. Is it an attitude, a perception or view of something or action? Is it a hurt unhealed or anger not diffused? Is it unforgiveness that we habour? Many would say I've done that going back over my life, why should I do it again? For me I want every nook and cranny swept clean. I don't want to leave any chance for the enemy to creep in bringing a drowsy state upon me. To continually inquire of the Lord, "Is there anything in my past you desire to take care of Father?" This shows a willing attitude of a child to submit to the Father, requiring His guidance and allowing Him into every aspect of our lives.

In a sense, what Father has done in our past becomes future opportunity to minister to others in similar areas.

It becomes the future of being able to remain awake, not drowsy. The knowledge we gain in the past becomes a teaching tool to aid others to deal with their past. It becomes a platform to where we can continue, advancing in our race with Christ to obtain the high calling that He has placed before us. Our past becomes our future in Christ, if we deal with it in now and with Him.

Acts 20:24 "But none of these things move me, neither count I my life dear unto myself, so that I might finish my course with joy, and the ministry, which I have received of the Lord Jesus, to testify the gospel of the grace of God."

"Heavenly Father I bless each one of us with the desire to deal with our past with & guided by your son, our Saviour, Jesus Christ. I bless each one of us to be equipped to make our past our future in you Lord. So, we may say with the saints: "I have fought the good fight, I have finished the race, I have kept the faith." 2 Timothy 4:7" Amen.

"Thank you, Heavenly Father."

HIS RIGHTEOUSNESS

I wish I could say this a little more chipper this morning. Father began speaking to me this morning at 3:30am, and as much as I requested that I be allowed to go back to sleep, here I am at 4:30am typing.

So many thoughts are going through my mind, but I shall try to weave them together as directed.

I am a procrastinator at times, putting off doing certain things till it is more convenient for me. Like this morning and Saturday as an example. It is with mixed sadness that I have to report that the young lady I ministered to two Saturdays ago has decided not to continue. I should have not been surprised but was disappointed.

Heavenly Father, knows the desire in my heart, to see people grasp your freedom plus live in it. But in saying that I know He is in all things, there is always hope. I had prayed and asked Him what He wanted to do. I didn't really get anything, and that which I did... well I procrastinated at pursuing. I laid in bed early Saturday praying receiving the scripture Romans 10. I put of reading till after I got up, then I chatted with Leroy on the phone, I would read after that, I had to get ready I would read after that... so forth. I didn't read Romans till I returned home from chatting briefly with a Pastor and another friend, in the church parking lot, regarding the young lady not coming. If I had read prior I would have known and perhaps understood why she wouldn't come. Reading that passage brought a number of questions to mind.... verses 2 "For I can testify about them that they are zealous for God, but their zeal is not based on knowledge. 3 Since they did not know the righteousness that comes from God and sought to establish their own, they did not submit to God's righteousness. 4 Christ is the end of the law so that there may be righteousness for everyone who believes."

What questions came to mind were, where in my own life have I brought in my own righteousness. Now such thoughts can have three conclusions, 1 - down into self-condemnation, knowing I can achieve nothing and do not. 2 - down into self-righteousness, where I think I could achieve all but do not. 3 - Down the middle with Christ, leaning heavily on His arms asking to reveal those areas, repenting quickly for them and appealing for His assistance to get out of that which I have sinned.

It was Paul who said, "all have fallen short of the Glory of God." Therefore, I am not and cannot judge anyone for where they are, for I have fallen short as well. As acutely aware, as Paul was of the thorn in his flesh, so am I of mine. What I can do, is discern, and encourage. I can discern, how one has gotten to where they are or where they will be if they continue on the path they are. Encourage, through Christ to repent, separate from sin, return to Him and stand firm. It is not an easy task I know this. But, if we remain in seeking self-righteousness or justification of where we are at, doing that which we should not, then as time goes by, it is even harder to return to the beloved of our soul.

Verse 8-11 "The word is near you; it is in your mouth and in your heart," that is, the word of faith we are proclaiming: .... 11 As the Scripture says, "Anyone who trusts in him will never be put to shame."

There is the hope, once more to Paul's words, (interpreted by me), "that which I want to do I do not, but that which I do not wish to do I do." Everything will be ok, if I do this down the road. Where does the road end, which bend will we chose when it comes? I suggest, repent now and often, stay close to His righteousness as possible, always call upon His help to do so. Know this, He is always near, He walks beside you, He lays beside you, He sits beside you. He is not an absent God. Even though His throne is in the Heavenlies, He came to earth to be here with us. His promises, at the time of His earthly body's death, is still here today. He did and has sent us a comforter. Our Living God is our Father in Heaven, He is the Son whom died on the cross for us, He is the Holy Spirit who covers and comforts us. He is here in every thought we have. Our sorrows are His, our joys are His. He suffers when we turn, saying I desire to live in sin rather than accept your grace and return to you. His hope is always there extending itself to us, to take, returning to our walk, no matter if it is a few inches we have strayed away or miles.

I know some of you my friends are going through extremely hard times, ones where you may not see the end right now or His hope. I wish I could snap my fingers or say a prayer and have you out of it. All I can do is stand with you, beseeching God on your behalf.

"Lord you know all circumstances, those areas where ones who call upon Your name and seek their own righteousness. I ask that You bring them up short, move upon their eyes. their minds to see your righteousness, so they may turn back to You. We all suffer from time to time of this. And we stretch Your mercy and grace thin, to cover our short comings. Today I ask that You, would move on all our hearts, drawing us closer to you. None of us are too far away from You to hear from you, to know, to feel your presence. You are Yahweh, You are God. You are our beloved. You are here. Blessed be Your Name Lord." Amen.

Now I think I will return to bed, for the short thirty to forty five minutes left before leaving for work.

Jeremiah 10:2-10 "This is what the LORD says: "Do not learn the ways of the nations or be terrified by signs in the sky, though, the nations are terrified by them. 3 For the customs of the peoples are worthless; they cut a tree out of the forest, and a craftsman shapes it with his chisel.

4 They adorn it with silver and gold; they fasten it with hammer and nails so it will not totter. 5 Like a scarecrow in a melon patch, their idols cannot speak; they must be carried because they cannot walk. Do not fear them; they can do no harm nor can they do any good." 6 No one is like you, O LORD; you are great, and your name is mighty in power. 7 Who should not revere you, O King of the nations? This is your due. Among all the wise men of the nations and in all their kingdoms, there is no one like you. 8 They are all senseless and foolish; they are taught by, worthless, wooden idols. 9 Hammered silver is brought from Tarshish and gold from Uphaz. What the craftsman and goldsmith have made is then dressed in blue and purple— all made by skilled workers. 10 But the LORD is the true God; he is the living God, the eternal King. When he is angry, the earth trembles; the nations cannot endure his wrath."

KNOWING WHO

Where did September go? I blinked and it went from August into October.

I got up really early today, the #1 bus past me as I made my way to the stop, but it was the #1 that is before the early #113, which is usually full.

A question arose in me last night of how many people are there sitting in the church pews calling themselves Christians and who are not?

How many are walking around calling themselves Christians who have never given their lives to Christ nor know of who He really is? When I became a Christian, my parents questioned my commitment, putting it down to needing a "crutch" to get by in life. I knew then as I know now that He is more than a "crutch", He lifts me up. He carries me. I am glad I know that I need Him, I know He is there for me, I can go to Him, I am glad He is my "crutch".

My mom asked me one day what I thought a Christian was, I told her, sadly she got upset, because that description did not fit who she was for she thought herself a Christian. She proclaimed she was a Christian because she lived in a Christian Nation. Being who I am I made some phone calls, did you know that Canada, US nor Britain are not listed as Christian nations? In fact, there are only five countries in the world, according to the United Nations, three are in Africa and two in South America. When I relayed her the information, she was furious.

Good News though my mom did accept the Lord a couple years before she died. Did she live a Christian life from that point on, no, but that is between Heavenly Father and her. She said the sinner's prayer and accepted the Lord into her heart.

Through the years I have meet others who have said that they are Christians, upon quizzing I found that they have never made a commitment, some didn't know who Christ really was. They dabble with things that they should not, some in lighter stuff like pagan worship, some go further into the occult. They wonder why things are not going well for them. Why they are dogged by demons, they are unable to dispose of or a heavy black cloud that will never lift. I have come to realize that I cannot call them brother or sister, for they are truly not of the same Faith in Christ that I am.

What do I do? Do I turn from them? Jude says no – Jude 1:22 "Be merciful to those who doubt; 23 snatch others from the fire and save them; to others show mercy, mixed with fear—hating even the clothing stained by corrupted flesh."

It can be a perplexing situation. I feel with those who are calling, themselves Christians and are not, and have not made a commitment to Christ should be told, as Christ directs, to the why's they should commit.

A situation came to my mind, this is due to a request to work with someone who refers to themselves as a Christian and feels they always has been. There has been no prayer of salvation, on their part plus they dabble in witchcraft naively. To rebuke them would shatter them, so Holy Spirit must direct. The first step is to lead them in a salvation prayer to a commitment to Christ, from that point on one can speak into their life and minister more effectively.

Jude 1 verse 20 "But you, dear friends, build yourselves up in your most holy faith and pray in the Holy Spirit. 21 Keep yourselves in God's love as you wait for the mercy of our Lord Jesus Christ to bring you to eternal life."

God Bless

What is true love?

1. Would you lay down your life for a loved one?
2. Would you forgive the one you love no matter what he or she has done to you?
3. Would you go out of your way to find your best friend that loves you so deeply?
4. Would you go down on your knees and ask your Father to forgive them for what they have done?
5. Would you let yourself go through all sorts of pain and punishment for your loved ones?
6. Could you raise yourself up from the grave for your loved ones?
7. Would you build a place with a whole lot of rooms just for the ones that you loved so deeply?

Guess what Jesus did this and a lot more just for you.

Let's remember to thank Jesus for all he has done for use.

"Dear Heavenly Father, I like to take this time and thank you for all you have done for me. I know I don't deserve it but you did it through the love that you have for me so I could be at your side one of these days up in heaven with you. I always will love you with all, of my heart and soul and try to walk the path you have laid before me. Thank you, Jesus." Amen and Amen

Mark 10: 22-23 "At this the man's face fell. He went away sad, because he had great wealth. 23 Jesus looked around and said to his disciples,

"How hard it is for the rich to enter the kingdom of God!" (for those who trust in riches)"

NO MAKEUP

I sort of surprised myself this morning…no it wasn't when I looked in the mirror either. It was when I was standing at the bus stop. Never do I leave the house without makeup on. I had bad sunburn years ago that left my facial skin always looking like I have a rash, and in these later years I have also developed rosacea which causes break outs. I was told by a dermatologist, that a person who did not have bad skin during teenage hood usually developed rosacea. I was one of those kids.

On my way, down town, I thought there must be something in this, some kind of story.

When I read the scriptures, He laid on my heart, I was a little puzzled. Is it about us wearing masks? It was when I reread the scripture, I saw something more there. I hope I can convey in a logical manner what I am sensing.

In Mark 10 Jesus is talking with a young rich man. We know the story, even though he wants to follow Christ, he turns away when Christ asks him to give all his money away. We all need money to function; that is the way it has been for centuries upon centuries. All have struggled from one point or another with our Christian prospective of how financial things work in our lives. Where the mask comes in is how we try to hide our concept of this dilemma, not just from others but from ourselves also. We say "If I were to win that jackpot, then I would give this to the church or charity or do this or that for Christ".

I know, you know, what I am talking about.

There is nothing wrong in thinking that, but how does it affect us? We live in the reality of not having enough funds in what we try to imagine.

The mask becomes poverty; we focus on the lack of our wants and our needs rather than on His provision. There is so much more I could

43

add to this going off in a spin about what lays in our backgrounds that affect our lack. But that is not the focus, even though it would be very interesting to explore.

Back to the real topic; masks and money.

I have personally, found it difficult at times to wear the mask of financial comfort, especially when there is a deep lack. I have learned to stretch a dollar to its limits. Even though I am inconsistence in my tithing, the Lord has blessed me greatly. I think the reason I wore that particular mask is because I didn't want to be pitied or thought ill of or self sufficient. I have been like that when a few negative comments were made to me about single parents. So, should I have worn a mask? Or wear one in the future? And how do I balance this with my seeking a deeper walk with Christ? I think the first step is being real with God first, then myself. Money does affect us, whether we have a lot or a little. Money does contribute to how I interact with others, whether I extend a helping hand or keep a tight grip on what I have. It also can affect my heart's desire to follow Christ if I allow it to. Christ continually asks me what am I willing to give, extend your hand, and do this with what you have in your pocket. At any point, I could say no and turn away, like the young wealth man, thinking the price, He has requested…is too high for me to pay. Will, I give all that I have financially to walk after Him? Do you know my character? It would be a difficult thing but I pray I would. He has put me in the situation a few times, the first was when both of my kids were about to get married, a month apart. I had been laid off from my short-term contract position with a land company when the oil industry was going through a slump. No jobs, my government employment insurance had run out and what little I had put aside was close to being gone as well. I had to be thrifty plus creative in order to get things for my kid's weddings. When I cried out to Heavenly Father, "why, why, why?" His reply was I need someone on the front of the plow. What could I learn from that position? And how did it relate to what I was facing at that moment in my life?

I learnt that the spirit of poverty is one we could accept or reject. How we reject it is how we view our situation through Christ. "Lord, it is a challenge for me to be in this situation but I am waiting to see how you will bless me in it." He did, with a job, though not in my field, but it was a job I could do and earn money at. A harder situation came 2007. Once more I had no job, EI was dragging its feet, and I had zilch for money. How did God bless me then? With my fiancé extending his finances to me. That was even more difficult! Not only that, but also my church extending their hand as well. Through this I learned more than one thing;

1-My mind had to make an adjustment from "single" thinking to "married" status. No, we hadn't married yet, but I saw God shifting my independency to – no not co-dependent – but inter-dependent way of thinking.

2- My depression had hit its all-time low; I felt the stress of having literally no money at all and seeing no prospect of employment. The spirit of poverty pressed hard on me. I had a choice, I didn't just have to accept and buckle under. Would I, could I, rise against and above it? The money aspect is a small part of the denominator; it is our perspective on the matter. I am rich in Christ. His promises are always there and fulfilled. God did not promise me riches; He promised me that I would always have a roof over my head and food to eat. He has always provided this. Even if it was questionable at times and lean, He kept to His promise. He is always nudged me to look at that which He had given and not comparing it to what the "world" sees as necessity.

What shall my mask be?

It should reflect He who is faithful and awesome. It should reflect that it is transparent in its composition in nature to show forth His truth, with no hidden agenda.

I hope that I have made sense.

God Bless.

Matthew 5:34-37 "But I tell you, Do not swear at all: either by heaven, for it is God's throne; 35or by the earth, for it is his footstool; or by Jerusalem, for it is the city of the Great King."

Unutterable Joy

It bothered me in a way to have written last Wednesday's story, Knowing Who, but such is the truth of this life. There are such people who call themselves Christians and are not.

2 Timothy 3:4 says "treacherous, rash, conceited, lovers of pleasure rather than lovers of God".

We see where their focus lays, and how connecting with them regularly can also affect our focus. I faced something similar these past few months, as I watched a dear friend turn their back on God because they felt He did not serve them well. The lack of providing as they put it was in the area job, home, children and a spouse. Ignoring what Heavenly Father had provided in their life, how He ministered to them, their focus was on earthly gratification and pleasure.

Heavy is the heart when one hears the words of a friend say, "I can't follow a God who doesn't care, any longer".

I had received a prophetic word for this individual before our last conversation, in it the Lord said..." they have turned from me and thus turned from my children." Having a conversation with this person was difficult as they maligned our Heavenly Father in bitterness and lies.

It reminds me of a book I read of a dream someone had, where they saw in a vision demons riding on the backs of Christians defecating and throwing up on them. The Christians they saw had a solution to get rid of the demons but they chose not to take it, ultimately, they became a weapon against the brothers and sisters they had once walked with.

I had hoped that when I read the scripture the Lord gave me this morning the topic would have been a lighter one. As I reflect upon Him, quizzing Him, He shows me the lightness of it. We are to heed these warnings of things that can happen. We are to be wise as serpents and gentle as doves. But in this wisdom, we are also to discern whom will be healthy to have in our lives and who would not be. I can understand frustration with God, in His lack of answering us at times or events happening that seem opposite of what we have comprehended. Who among us have not been there? Paul with many of his brethren were beaten, jailed, murdered because of their faith in Christ. Would they have not also felt the same frustration? How can we think our lives should be better then theirs in wealth, and material objectives? None the less, they continued to seek God's face, believing in Christ and eventually were inspired by Holy Spirit to see the revelation of the Lord's mercy and grace.

Whom am I, Lord? We see in Matthew 5, that God is every where, all is His. This is where our focus should be. This is where the lightness comes in, the hope of knowing something better. One may say, I do not have a good job, but let me praise Him in what I do have. Let me seek His face in that which He has provided me. As I write this down, I can not say I have always done this, easier to grumble to God. Yet, through Leroy and my frustrations over not being able to get married in either country, we encourage each other to seek God, to look past the walls our governments seem to erected. I saw on a woman's jacket back the other day printed Misery. How sad, how sad that she would want to live under that when there is an opportunity to live in a joy that is unspeakable. To live in Christ, to seek His peace, His joy, His love in a life that is wracked with turmoil is a feat indeed, however my dear friends it holds unbelievable fulfillment one can not express in words.

"God give me words to encourage my friends to look up. Only You, Holy Spirit, moving upon their hearts and minds can fill them with Father's words. Let it be today, so they can take each step forward deeper into Christ."

Blessed be your days my friends. As we celebrate Thanksgiving here in Canada, let us seek in our lives' areas where we are Thankful to Father. I, thank you Lord, that I have these friends, who have encouraged me, uplifted me and stood by me. Even when they didn't think they did. Thank you that you have healed wounds so we can go forward together with each other even if it is miles apart. Yes, Lord I hear your angels rejoicing, for this is Your day, with us individually. Manifest yourself Jesus in a special way to each one of us, so we are encouraged that You are Truth in us. Amen.

1 Peter 5:8 "Be self-controlled and alert. Your enemy the devil prowls around like a roaring lion looking for someone to devour. 9Resist him, standing firm in the faith, because you know that your brothers throughout the world are undergoing the same kind of sufferings. 10And the God of all grace, who called you to his eternal glory in Christ, after you have suffered a little while, will himself restore you and make you strong, firm and steadfast"

YOUR DAY

How have your days been my friends?

How has your walk with Christ been going?

Mine have not been heavy but they have not been light either. I ponder some things a lot, then others that I should ponder, I desire not to think of.

I read the scripture that I felt lead to read today, Jeremiah 20. Jeremiah is in quite the state here, cursing the day he was born and trying to turn away from the Lord, yet knowing in his heart he can not. I would say he was having a bad day. I am sure many of us have had similar days where we question God to the why were we born, mostly during our times of misery. However, Jeremiah was able to squeak out, "Sing to the LORD! Give praise to the LORD! He rescues the life of the needy from the hands of the wicked." in verse 13. Upon reading 1 Peter 5:8-10 though I felt the assurance of the Lord. Peter mentions that other brothers and sisters around the world are going through the same. Some to a deeper degree of having to stand for their faith then we are here on the North American continent. I know that doesn't eliminate the burden you are under. But take solace in it. Others are struggling, others are crying out to God like Jeremiah centuries ago, "Why was I born to go through such things?"

What is there to take heart of? A couple of things for now, He has called you to His Eternal Glory in Christ. He will himself restore you and make you strong, firm, and steadfast.

It is a positive note to take hold of, once more a promise from Him. He has called you, He will restore you.

I would like to share a dream I had a few years back.

"It was dusk, in the foreground I see ruins of buildings in a field. Among the ruins stood figures clothed in long robes. I don't remember any colours.

They stood not close together but distance between them. They were facing away from a hill was that behind them. A man appeared on a horse from behind the hill advancing to the crest of it. Then others joined him. They were intent on killing the people that stood below, as they rode down the hill, they jeered and antagonized the standing figures. They rode circles around the standing figures. Drawing their swords, they were ready to strike at any moment. The robed figures did not move nor did they raise their heads. They seemed unmoved by what was going on around them. As the riders raised their arms to strike down the ones they taunted the robed figures suddenly revealed and swung large swords. The swiftness of the movement even startled me in the dream. They all moved at the same time, without hesitation. The blow was so swift that the riders were caught off guard becoming the victims of death themselves. Upon waking from the dream, the Lord

49

spoke, saying that we, Christians, should be like those robed figures, sure in our faith in Christ. A word of encouragement to be prepared in Him, that when He commands we will act with swiftness and force. We are to be immersed in the Lord, so the enemy will not rattle us with his taunting's.

Bless you with the Lord our Jesus Christ's move upon your life as He prepares you.

Galatians 2:3-5 But neither Titus, who was with me, being a Greek, was compelled to be circumcised: 4 And that because of false brethren unawares brought in, who came in privily to spy out our liberty which we have in Christ Jesus, that they might bring us into bondage: 5 To whom we gave place by subjection, no, not for an hour; that the truth of the gospel might continue with you.

1 Corinthians 7:22-24 For he who was a slave when he was called by the Lord is the Lord›s freedman, similarly, he who was a free man when he was called is Christ›s slave. 23 You were bought at a price, do not become slaves of men. 24 Brothers, each man, as responsible to God, should remain in the situation God called him to.

BEING FREE

Can you believe this, not only is another week drawing to a close so is another month?

Wow, eh! I still haven't found what happened to September, yet. I think I should rename the early #113 bus to the regular #113, for I seem to be able to catch it quite frequently now.

There is quite the social gathering that goes on in that bus. At the front, there are three ladies in their mid to later fifties, two of them have thick British accents, and a single mom with her seven or eight year old son.

The last couple of days the little boy has read from a joke book he got from his school library. The older women were quite amused, sending up gales of laughter.

At the back of the bus, a mother and her twenty something daughter sit. Last week they had quite the row about paying rent. My feeling was they should keep that stuff at home for it is not a public issue.

Another young mother with a six-year-old daughter comes on the bus, sitting where they can find a seat. Today they sat beside me on the mid-section side bench. The girl sang a little song all the way to their stop. It made me smile.

The one person I don't miss on the morning commute is the fellow in his early twenties, who plays his CD with his headphones hanging about his neck, the tinny sound of the music carries all the way to the front.

The bus driver is quite chipper, he is an East Indian man in his mid-thirties, always has a smile on his face. He knows who gets on his bus and will wait a few seconds for some, if they are a little late. I like taking the bus at this time, it gets me to work about 7:15am so I have time to look up scriptures, pray a little, and say good morning to Leroy on my cell phone.

When I arrived at work, today, I asked for a scripture and received the above two. I thought about the ones on the bus, other people as well as myself. It is interesting how this freedom of ours can be taken out of context and misinterpreted. Nor is this freedom always understood. When I was working at a larger oil company while my kids were in their mid-teens, I had a small breakdown. I say small because I only took two months off to recuperate. I was pursuing a career, that was my focus, that is how I was defining my life and identity. I was a "teen" in Christ at the time, meaning I was still an immature Christian, not referring to age wise. I prayed and pressed the Lord for some kind of answer, what insight I received was "they want your soul." Reminds me of that song Tennessee Ernie Ford use to sing, "Sixteen Tons" with the lyrics "I owe my soul to the company store." I realized then, that is the devotion company's want from their employees. They want to be the center of one's life, their heart beat. Yes, we should be good, honest workers. How far do we take this devotion? Who is the center of our lives? Our employers are not the only ones that compete with Christ for the center seat in our soul. When we have that freedom in Christ, which is to see, respond and envision Him in our lives, outside sources do not like it. Others come to us with rules and regulations not based on the scriptures. They guilt us, selling us a bill of goods into becoming slaves. I sound like a little rebel, don't I? I am not trying to be, but something precious is at stake. Something that the scriptures have addressed which we should also take inventory in our lives concerning it. Yes, our jobs can be very demanding, very stressful, but does that mean we should be putting in twelve hour days, week after week, without voicing something? I know it is not an easy situation to be in, especially for those who work shifts. What are the downfalls of it? Have you approached Heavenly Father on a solution of it? Our society for eons have pressed us into slavery. At of recent years we can be coined as not being a team player if we don't bow to the move of the general masses, even though we could be better workers then that majority. Is it prevalent in the Christian movement, where there are a series of hoops present, not Biblically based, to jump through before we can obtain that which Christ died for to give to us freely? Once, the Lord directed me to give my tithe to a friend who had lost her job. I did that for two months, basically supporting her and her daughter for that time. Without it she would not have survived, ending up on the streets. After, I returned to give the tithe to the church I was attending. The pastor visited me concern on this matter, I shared what I felt the Lord had me do. He disagreed, feeling that I should have given her monies over and above the tithe. I expressed I could not afford that. A couple of Sundays after that he gave a series of lectures on tithing, bolding saying that the widow who gave her last mite had not given enough. I left the church at that point. No, I am not saying you should not tithe, nor that you should look to some other place to put it outside the congregation you are attending. What I am saying is that I had a freedom to follow after God's lead, putting my tithe money where He chose. It is not always so cut and dry, though is it? I am not saying that the pastor was totally wrong either, however, I feel he was bound by his traditional concept of tithing and allowing it to imprison him.

Maybe I am wrong on this.

The point, I wish to convey is there are those who have entered into our surroundings on the pretense of presenting Biblical "options", when it is our freedom in Christ that they are desiring to steal from us. I am going to bring up another point, attending church, do I do that faithfully? No. But why is it important to attend a church? One is, the fellowship with likeminded believers, Secondly, iron sharpens iron. We need a place where they can offer to us other possible ways to view what God is presenting us, plus they need to hear other options as well. Some of those options you may hold. As we fellowship and share we can ponder these things with the scriptures and in prayer. Chances could be both hold the wrong view and both can be corrected. Thirdly, a chance to receive ministry as well as practice it.

Now as I have shared all these I am aware that they all have loopholes as well as what ifs. My fourth point on church attendance is it draws a unity with those who are seeking after the Living God of Israel, our Lord Jesus Christ. We need that these days. We need to know there are others about us who are struggling too, some who have been strengthened both can share insights to that strengthening. We need to know that there are those in the world who are slave hunters who will take no mercy in taking us captive. We can retain our freedom by watching and fellowshipping with others who have freedom in Christ. We can be strengthened to be aware of the wiles of the enemy and to avoid many of them, hopefully all.

My encouragement is, firstly seek the Lord on your freedom situation right now, are you a slave or a free man. Ask Him what areas in your live are you enslaved. Press Him to show you how He would like to free you. Above all things, make sure it is Jesus Christ who answers you. The answers should be logical and biblically based. Not our flight of fancy to get out of working on a Christian marriage you think is one-sided. If you feel this is the case, seek good Christian counselling, requesting your spouse do as well, and together.

Sorry, long story.

Be blessed today.

Psalm 139:1

You have searched me, LORD, AND YOU KNOW ME.

Discrimination happens among us

Today, the topic is a little more sobering. No giggling babies, bus tours, or getting lost, but my little tale does come from my bus ride into the city center. I asked God how to tackle this subject, His reply, even though subtle, was, "head on".

Prejudice is on every level in our society. No matter who you are or where you are or how you live, it's there.

As I watched some people get on the bus, I saw a man clothed in grubby jeans, sweat shirt and carrying a dirty cooler, obviously he was a construction worker. That's when the topic hit me.

What is our first reaction when we look at people? I remember an incident, a number of years ago, when I was returning to the oil industry after my year sabbatical, I started work at a geological mapping company. The first appointment was to take over on the call-in desk.

My attitude, "who me!" I was a geophysical / geological technician who use to be the call-in client. My first day there I reached out my hand to turn the door handle, Heavenly Father spoke very loudly to me, "You are quite the snot aren't you!" Can a person change their whole demeanor in a split second? It is possible, for when I stepped through that door I was changed. His word to me cut me so quickly and deeply that it changed me immediately.

Who Am I? Who Am I!

Discrimination happens among Christians, us believers, it may be subtle or pronounced but it is there. We allow it to affect our judgment of people and how we minister. It is only by the grace of God that I am not a street person, for I have come close a couple of times to being homeless. His mercy and grace is beyond my comprehension. We think of those street people, who have come out of hard situations as success stories, but are they to God? Perhaps their success story was how they ministered His Word and Life to those whom they were among.

I know to the business people around me, I was not a success, especially when I did not share.

Perhaps it is the same with you.

Jesus, walked and dined among the down trodden of His time, He still does in our time. Am I suggesting we dine with a street person, no, but if Father leads you that way then humble yourself not only to do it but also in your attitude. See them in His Truth, some street people He wouldn't want you to dine with either, but He will show you if or when it is to be done. Mean time minister where you are.

Who Am I? When I went to work as a house keeper-companion I found it difficult at first. It took God a month to change my perspective. Now my attitude now is "How can I bless 'them' Lord with You", meaning those I work with. Do I have to get on my soap box and preach? No, but seeking Him constantly asking what can I do... that's it. I cannot look at someone who is dressed differently then I and judge their character for they may be more of a success story then I. God's grace may be resting on their shoulders heavier than on mine for I don't have to face what they do right now.

> Not because of who I am
> But because of what you have done
> Not because of what I have done
> But because of who You are
> Who Am I, a song by Casting Crowns taken from Ps 139
> Take a minute, read the Psalm.
> God Bless you

John 3:16 "For God so loved the world that he gave his one and only Son, that whoever believes in him shall not perish but have eternal life

1 John 3:16 This is how we know what love is: Jesus Christ laid down his life for us. And we ought to lay down our lives for our brothers.

Looking Up

Today is going to be a difficult story to write, but I feel Heavenly Father's nudging and I pray that what I share will help many, if not all of you.

The topic is depression. Depression in itself, is not difficult for me, it is the story Father encourages me to relate. I had struggled with it most of my life, as a child, a teen and into my adulthood. I have found something, though, that helps me in abating these dark moods. This tool has been developed over years of listening, searching information and prayer, basically, bugging the heck out of Heavenly Father. I will start by sharing that I was married the first time for two years around thirty-two years ago. I was in my late teens, we had two wonderful kids, whom both of us love deeply. Raising my kids on my own was a "challenging" task. I was a strict mom, too strict perhaps. When my kids were still quite young I gave my life to Christ and began my trek as a follower of Christ. Over the years I have experienced a lot. At first, I struggled and dated, but then at one point rededicated my life in a more serious manner to the Lord resigning myself to the fact that I was going to be single for life. It wasn't till about eight years ago that I felt that the Lord had someone special for me. I did start looking. I met a few fellows who said they were serious; a couple of them meant it, but not really in the way that I did. I thought I had found the one I was to spend my life with twice, only to find out, not. Depression hit hard both times. I was angry and upset at God, for promises, then they were cruelly being snatched away. Before I met Leroy, I had bitterly told God that His men were jerks and if the ones I had met were examples He could keep them. I apologize for any offence, but that is how I felt. Oh, I respected and still respect my male friends, but the ones who expressed their so-called commitment to me well I had to work at it. These were actually nice fellows and would make wonderful friends. But with each, they were intrigued with my spirituality and couldn't handle the rest. They always said I was "different", not bad different, just different, whatever that means, but no real excuse to end a relationship. Yes, I have forgiven them and have moved on, thank you, Lord, for helping me. There is the brief synopsis of my background.

About the time I met Leroy, I had given up on a relationship for I felt Father had played "jokes" on me with the other ones, so I didn't want any more. Ha, ha, ha... I think my weird sense of humour, keeps me in the barely sane category, though many would want to debate that issue. To make the story short and get to the point, after a few months of Leroy pursuing me I did allow myself to fall in love with him. Who is a very remarkable fellow, and accepts every part of me plus can handle me! Mmmm... Most of you know the events that have followed regarding our marriage and now our visa waiting period. On the way, back from the Vancouver border, I was very angry with God and yelled a lot of stuff at Him. Mostly accused Him of playing, yet again, the sick joke of giving me something then yanking it away at the last minute. And yes, depression did rear its ugly head. As I have learned over the years, if one side steps this menace then one only prolongs the process of it hanging around. I now have gotten to the point where I met things head on, lay it before the Lord and work through it. It is not an easy process but this method cleanses one of any past loopholes that the enemy sneaks in on, seals them up, exposes any short comings that are flaws in our persona which may invite the enemy to play havoc in our lives. Plus the added bonus, we gain a deeper understanding of our loving, wonderful Creator, our Heavenly Bridegroom. It is this process that aids in the dispersion of depression from us. Look at the situation that you are in, state everything you see about it, even if it is all the negatives to God and what you feel about them. Rant and rave if you need to. Then sit down, saying "God what do you say?" Write down everything that comes into your head, everything. Holding each up to the Lord saying, "what gives or what do you say Lord?" Keep in mind what Christ did for you. I feel that John. 3:16 is not just for the nonbelievers for them to come to Christ, but it is the bases of our foundation in Him. This needs to be re-enforced continually because the enemy will persist to buffet it. Cry, like there is no tomorrow, don't hold it in; sob your little heart out before God. Then ask yourself, "Why do I really feel this way?" Examine each thing. I had to examine why I felt God was playing a joke on me. It went way back to my childhood of how my brother treated me. I had to forgive him, and God, for doing that to me, making me feel that way, even if God didn't do it, I still had to forgive Him. I then asked for forgiveness in having that thought and allowing it to taint my perceptions of Him. With the trip home from Vancouver, I did a lot of forgiving, I was deflated, embarrassed. I am not now. God has made me focus in on Him and has given me something to encourage others to focus in on Him. Do I cry over Leroy's and my situation, yep, I do. Then I thank Him for His perfect love, grace and mercy. Through my pain, He has allowed something wonderful to happen, to blossom. It is not of me, it is totally of Christ. EL ROI - God Who opens our eyes. JEHOVAH-SHAMMAH - Lord is There.

The enemy would like us to believe God plays cruel jokes on us, that He has abandoned us, thus with these thoughts he spirals us deeper into the abyss of depression.

God does not play jokes, He has not abandoned us, He stands beside us, He holds us in His arms, He is there (here).

Confront the demon of your depression, lift it up to God, lay it before Him as you both examine it together, grieve it, allow God's healing to come as you press into His word of who He is in Truth, stand in His light for His mercy covers you in cleansing, receive His healing and most of all look up into His eyes.

"Father, You, know what besets us to bring us down, making us cast our eyes upon the sorrow of our souls. You, know why we get stuck in the living of that misery, but You have given us something to get out of it, Christ Your Son, our Lord. It is a difficult trek to rise out of it but what a wonderful journey, and what an awesome ascent into Your waiting embrace. I ask, Father, this day for all my friends, and those who read this, that You would extend Your mercy and love upon them when the enemy tries to bring them down into despair. Raise them up Father, lift their head to gaze into Your eyes, Your hope, and Your life. Amen."

John 3:13-16

13 No one has ever gone into heaven except the one who came from heaven—the Son of Man. 14 Just as Moses lifted up the snake in the desert, so the Son of Man must be lifted up 15 that everyone who believes in Him may have eternal life. 16 For God so loved the world that He gave His one and Only Son, that whoever believes in Him shall not perish

but have eternal life. 17 For God did not send His Son into the world to condemn the world, but to save the world through him."

New Light

Heavenly Father laid this scripture upon my heart this morning as I was getting ready to go to work.

As I made it to the bus stop, one of the regular ladies who takes the #113 was coming down the other hill. I saw her in a different light as verse 16 came back to mind. I greeted the lady by saying "good morning.", then mentioned I was late yesterday. This opened it up to our conversing a little more as we waited. On the bus at another stop one of the other ladies got on joining in the conversation.

"God so loved the world." How amazing, that He could bring into our eyes a different way to perceive people. Even the street person who hugged the minute corner of the bus shelter from the rain today. God has counted the hairs on his head too, as He has numbered the grains of sand on a beach. I tingle inside at the prospect of coming to know this love in a deeper way every day.

As Christians we tend to, not forget, as much as it has grown stale or have a common place in our lives, the knowledge of this love. Through the busyness of our daily lives and desire to "work" at our Christianity, the reality of having a Heavenly Bridegroom anxiously waiting for us, is dim. His passion for us. His longing to have us know Him burns deeper in Him then when 'we' first fell in love with Him.

"That He gave His one and only Son".

An omnipresent, awesome God gave us His Son. He approved of us to come to know His Son, to worship and adore Him, to be His bride.

Wow, eh! Wow.

That Our God approved of us way before we acknowledged His existence. So that we may fellowship with the only One who has come to earth. then returned to the Heavenly realm.

"For God so loved the world"

I cannot explain what change has taken place, it is hard to fathom it myself, but I know it has happened. Will I be running out & preaching the Word on the streets? Mmm...nay... but when I look at someone, as like this morning, I see them differently now. It was head knowledge, I knew God loved the world, I knew He sent His Son into the world to save it. I knew this, but something has changed where I see it. Yep, I am grinning.

"Lord, I ask that You, will change our perception of people. How is it God how You see them? Let us see them as You do, through Your heart, with Your wisdom and knowledge, so we may be Your hands and feet, Father as You have ordained us to be. Heavenly Father, I ask for a very special favor today for my friends who read this, that You would touch their hearts with Your kiss so they may feel at this moment Your rush of love for them. Let every day with You, Lord, be like the very first time we fell in love with You. I know You have always loved us. Thank you for that. Thank you for allowing us to fall in love with You. I bless each friend with that joy I am feeling right now, Father. Envelope them in it, wash them in it, drench them in it, Jesus. So when the storm comes they can lean on the calming of Your Love in their hearts. Thank you for this day and everyone that follows You, even when we face something where we don't really want to thank You for. Lord, You, are truly awesome. Amen."

Malachi 2:3 "Because of you I will rebuke your descendants; I will spread on your faces the offal from your festival sacrifices, and you will be carried off with it.

(offal - 1 : the waste or by-product of a process: as a : trimmings of a hide b : the by-products of milling used especially for stock feeds c : the viscera and trimmings of a butchered animal removed in dressing)

1 Peter 2:8-10 8and, "A stone that causes men to stumble and a rock that makes them fall." They stumble because they disobey the message—which is also what they were destined for. **9But you are a chosen people, a royal priesthood, a holy nation, a people belonging to God, that you may declare the praises of him who called you out of darkness into his wonderful light.** 10Once you were not a people, but now you are the people of God; once you had not received mercy, but now you have received mercy.

Royal Priesthood

I received the above scripture yesterday, before I started work in the morning I was typing up a story, but my day got quite busy from 7:30am till 4pm, leaving time.

Last night I couldn't sleep even though I tried, sleep didn't till about 1:30-2am, when I woke up this morning it was like I had hit a brick wall. I remember coughing through the time I did sleep, rising out of bed shaky. I called in sick resting most of the morning. It didn't dawn on me till mid-morning that this was the day I was to start praying, then of course it made a little sense to me. I went to my computer checking all my e-mails responding to Season of prayer story. Asked for a scripture this morning, Matthew 10:12 (As you enter the home, give it your greeting.)

"What do I do with this Lord?" "Pray"

"My readers, I have entered into your home, you have invited me. I thank you for that. I greet you in the Name of our Lord Jesus Christ who loves you and cares for you and has sent me this day to pray for you. Even though it may seem like a blanket prayer, take it to heart for it is meant for you, as if He gave it to me just for you specifically. For He sits beside you right at this moment, even though the enemy whispers in your ears his lie of saying God has abandoned you. He has not. Through every black moment He sits, stands and moves with you. You are His Royal Priesthood. Even though Halloween has past there are other festivals that come and we, as His priesthood, should be careful in how we partake of them. Ask Heavenly Father to look beyond what the world presents, to the essence of His heart on the matter. For as His priesthood we have a responsibility to our children and our children's children, to our neighbors, to our brothers and sisters in Christ. These are hard times, no less but more than those in the past."

"Heavenly Father you know what each of us face in our lives. Today, I ask for strength, your strength. Some of us cannot take another step forward for we have been sorely pressed down. Thank you, Father, for extending your arm for us to lean on, your arm of strength, we are Your Royal priesthood. We are not worthy of this position, but we are in it as we have stepped forward into relationship with You. We have struggled to maintain our place in Your light, all odds have come against us. We have stumbled, yet, You have reached out Your hand to steady us. At times Lord, it doesn't seem that your hand is there, but it is. Today, I ask for Your strength in each of our lives, to steady our feet, to steady our minds on you, to steady our beings. Strengthen us, Lord, in each of the areas that we need. Father, let this request go beyond words, let it be born on Your Words, as You breathe visible and renewable strength into us. Thank you, Father."

Matthew 26

SURPRISE GIFT GIVEN

People who are not familiar with Calgary's weather or have not experienced it first hand would find it rather hard to believe how fast the temperatures can change here, though not as dramatic as they had in the past. When, I was growing up and into my thirties, a Calgary winter could produce -30oC <-22oF> weather, then a Chinook wind would blow in, then the temperature could go up to +20oC <68oF>. A Chinook is a warm westerly wind that comes in from the Pacific Ocean up over the mountains into Alberta. Today we have a Chinook, the temperature change is not as I just described, but still nice. Yesterday we had -4oC <25oF> weather, today, it will be +13oC <56oF>, short sleeve weather. I wasn't expecting to be here for the winter and had packed away all my winter clothes. I packed my favorite jacket and boots in a box to leave at Dad's for when I came back to visit during the winter. For a couple of weeks, I have pondered on where I had put that box. Neither Dad nor I can remember what happened to it, we concluded it must be in the storage shed under my many waiting boxes.

As I stood at the bus stop after work last night, again I wondered about the box, I looked up, there was a woman walking down the street with my jacket on. How did I know that, and it wasn't one that just looked like it? I knew for I made it last year. I bought some fleece, sewed the jacket. The fleece is a white cream background with brown moose and green fir trees on it, a nice Canadian pattern. I lined it with brown fleece, buying special clasps to put on it for uniqueness. As I stood there amazed, trying to figure out how she had gotten it, plus deciding how I should feel about it. I recalled when I was moving that I had put aside some articles to send off to a charity. I had also separated this, particular box to one side, so who took the charity articles must have grabbed this box also. A small voice came to me in those few seconds as I pondered these things, saying, "Bless her." That I did, I blessed the lady with warmth, for the coat is a warm one. On the way home, I thought about the blessing and felt I had given a gift, though it was more of a surprise to me then it would have been for her.

Once more this morning it came to my mind, so I asked Heavenly Father for a scripture. He led me to Matthew 26, where the priests have transpired against Jesus, the woman pours the vile of alabaster on his feet, Judas betrays him and Peter denies him. Is the alabaster the only gift in these verses? No, there are many, if we wish to look beyond the words, into the essences of them. We see not only Jesus giving His life for us, but a feast prepared for us and redemption after we have turned from Him. I am sure there is more there. Though Christ was not surprised at the gift He gave us, it is the attitude in which He gave it we should learn to study and desire. Too many times I have heard that if I give something it would return to me ten-fold, even though Biblical, I have always felt it projects an expectation that taints the giving aspect. Did Jesus expect this upon His death? That all He sacrificed would be given back to Him ten-fold? His attitude and Heavenly Father's attitude were and are different from ours. They give for a purpose, a joy, a love in much of the time which we can not comprehend. Let us eagerly set our sights on such impartation of the understanding of this aspect, to become surprised givers.

"Heavenly, Father, today I wish to pray for our giving attitude along with our receiving attitude. First, I would like to ask for Your forgiveness on our past expectations in both areas, where we have given with an expectation of being rewarded and an expectation of receiving which may hinge on demand. We have been trained wrong, we have developed wrong expectations and presumptions, for this Father I ask that You forgive us, and through your grace teach us, reveal to us Your mindset on this. Father, let us give without thinking of anything but merely seeing a need and providing for it, no what if's or should be's, just merely to extend a hand to bless. Jesus, You did this for us, rightfully, if we desire to follow you, we should also be after Your concept of giving. Father, I ask also that You would change our attitude about receiving, there are times where we are in dire need to receive and there are those who you have sent to extend Your grace in giving to us. Let us not have an expectation of, "it should be done for us." Rather a joy in the situation and an even greater joy when receiving. Lord, it is difficult at times to receive, for we feel unworthy or too self-sufficient, adjust both attitudes, Father.

Lord, I now lift up my friends who are in situations of need, circumstances of life have placed them there and they do require intervention on Your part. I ask, Father, for Your favour that You would extend Your hand of mercy into these situations along with Your impartation of wisdom plus understanding. Thank you, Father. Amen"

THEY CALL ME MELLOW YELLOW

Do you remember that song of the late 60's, "they call me mellow yellow.. quite rightly" by Donavon. It's a catchy tune, written for an Amsterdam cannabis shop of the time where, rumor has it, they smoked dried banana leaves.

Only the word mellow is of interest in my story today.

I have been mellow these past few days, not sad or depressed just placid. It would not take much to make me cry, but it would be for no apparent reason that I would have tears. I did cry last week in the doctor's office, upset him a little, but after that I felt fine. I could look at my situation and feel quite defeated.

Leroy and I have been struggling to maintain a positive and optimistic outlook on things. That is why, to me, this morning's scripture seems important. I know the enemy in his arrogance dances with glee when things are not always going the direction we feel it should. He likes to throw wrenches into the works & way lay us in our earthly walk with Christ.

Louder still, to hear his chuckles of delight as we slump under sorrow and defeat.

I encourage you this day though, whatever you are facing, whether it is small or earth shattering. Lift your head and shout to God, "Raise me up Lord when mine enemy rejoices over me. Raise me up Lord when those the enemy has persuaded hate me with no cause to. Raise me up Lord and fill me with your joy, your victory."

I have a song on right now, "I am a friend of God, He calls me friend." sung by Israel Israel Houghton.

James 2: 23 And the scripture was fulfilled which saith, Abraham believed God, and it was imputed unto him for righteousness: and he was called the Friend of God.

If we are friends of God, if He does call us friend and much more, beloved children. Then He will fill us with joy. Look up it is raining outside. Go outside and look up asking Father for His rain. Rain of refreshing, rain of the joy that will surpass any sorrow. Rain of His love.

"Heavenly Father so many of us here are heavy laden with what the enemy has heaped on us. We are weary of the battle, yet the dawn is ahead of us. To make it Father we need that rain. Pour it down on us Lord. Cleanse us, refresh us, cover us Lord. We need it now Father. Avert our eyes from the defeatism, the lairs the enemy has set up before us; enable us to see You and only Your shining face, for You are close, Father. Closer then what we can imagine. Lift our hearts Father so we may dance, sing and rejoice, falling on our knees abandoned from fears and rejoice before you Lord, in the midst of our oppressor and his cohorts. Yeah Lord... amen."

Bless you this day.

Ephesians 1:2&12

2 Grace and peace to you from God our Father and the Lord Jesus Christ.

12 in order that we, who were the first to hope in Christ, might be for the praise of his glory.

WALKING CAREFULLY

Freezing rain began this early morning, making roads and sidewalks slick. So easy steps were required for careful walking.

My early #113 bus was late today because of the road condition. I thought I had missed it, but he arrived. I thank God for this fellow, I would have found it difficult driving a car, and here he is driving a large bus full of people.

"Heavenly Father, bless this young man with Your grace and if he doesn't know You as his personal Saviour, then I ask for a favour for him, that You would move upon his live so he can meet and join with You."

I asked Father last night what He wanted me to pray about and share today. I felt He wanted me to pray for Seniors, like my Dad and his girlfriend. As I asked Him for direction with the story and the scripture, I felt He desired me to share a little bit of my salvation testimony, a very brief portion.

How I came to know who Christ is due to the prayers of my maternal great grandparents. While alive they never spoke to me about Christ. Even though, their daughter, my grannie, taught me how to pray, she didn't relate to me about having a personal relationship with Jesus. During the pregnancy with my son, I knelt in her living room, not yet a nonbeliever and asked God if He would allow my kids to know who He was. I said I didn't know Him, but wanted my children to a choice in life. Three years later, a single parent of two, I gave my life to Christ. Upon receiving Him as my Saviour, I heard God reminding me of the prayer I had made years earlier. He said, "How can they know Me, if you don't?" Years later I learnt that my great grandparents had prayed for their grandchildren and their children.

As I pondered this event in my life this morning, about how Father was going to tie things together, I re-read Matthew 1:12. "in order that we, who were the first to hope in Christ, might be for the praise of His glory."

There are many stories I could relate that my grannie had shared with me after I became a Christian, about her parent's life, and some about who she was. That is not the focus today. Many, like me, do not or did not have "Godly" parents. My Mom accepted Christ close to her death, mainly through fear of what was going to happen to her. My dad is yet to come, though he tells people I am his spiritual councilor. He has thought for a long time that I was a pastor, because I went on ministry trips. The question then, is how can we see the practicality of that scripture with our unchristian parents... or yet to be's...we can't. Pondering, once again, Father inspired me to think of how we can be to them and how we are to view them. Watching loved ones age can be a challenging thing. Spry, once, full of ideas, adventurous, some have closed off their lives and find moving cumbersome, conversation with intelligence illusive. As we gaze at their faces we can see the pain, confusion and frustration there. We begin then to make the error of treating them as children, even though some act like it, we view them as lesser. As, Heavenly Father, reminded me this morning we must look beyond all that presents itself, seeking the person who they are or once were, to quiz them of their past life. It can be an "interesting journey" for them as well as for us. One day we will be there, wanting for someone to see the value in us. My generation, the North American's coin as baby boomers, are in a unique position. Not only can we, as Christians, speak into a generation who is passing but also into the future ones. It is here, where we must press into Heavenly Father for wisdom. As a friend has expressed in once about her biological parents, to be His light to them. What a marvelous opportunity.

"Heavenly Father what an interesting prayer for today. I ask that, You, would give me insight to how to specifically pray for what You, want me to. I ask that You, would give us Your eyes to see the older generation and as I type I am aware that I am that older generation to my children and grandchildren. I ask that You, would bless them with the ability to see me how You see me. In turn, for me to see my Dad, and other elder people, the way You see them. Let us see the treasure that You have created in them, help us to speak to that so they may blossom even more, especially now when they think they are withering. Breathe fresh life into them. Move upon their aged minds so they may see You and receive You. I remember years ago, Father, of that 60's something fellow who had just received You and in his sure delight of new life, he danced about saying it is never too late. What a joy for the elder in our lives who know You. For those who are not yet to receive; Father, let not this year pass without them knowing who You are and bowing before You to accept you and experience a deeper fullness of You. Bless our mouths to impart peace, encouragement, patience, and love to them. Now Father, bless us, so that we may be for the praise of Your glory, to bless the younger generations coming up. Thank you, Father, for this special prayer today."

Bless you all

Matthew 18: 2 He called a little child and had him stand among them. 3 And he said: "I tell you the truth, unless you change and become like

little children, you will never enter the kingdom of heaven. 4 Therefore, whoever humbles himself like this child is the greatest in the kingdom of heaven.

"What I like about 'CHANGE' is that it's a synonym for "HOPE". What you are really saying is, 'I BELIEVE IN TOMORROW & I WILL BE PART OF IT.'.....Linda Ellerbee – US Broadcast Journalist

Hebrews 6: 18 God did this so that, by two unchangeable things in which it is impossible for God to lie, we who have fled to take hold of the hope offered to us may be greatly encouraged. 19 We have this hope as an anchor for the soul, firm and secure. It enters the inner sanctuary behind the curtain, 20 where Jesus, who went before us, has entered on our behalf. He has become a high priest forever, in the order of Melchizedek.

Hope within the Change – 01/16/07

The last 3 days I have mused over this topic, for I have always desired what I write is Heavenly Father's words and not just my prattling.

Responses to my stories have greatly encouraged me when you have shared your personal battles and prayers. Many times I have pondered to Jesus, "what hope can I share?"

When in prayer, I have pleaded for Him to show forth His mercy & reveal Himself in your situations.

I think of my son and my oldest grandson.

Is there hope?

Proverbs 13:12 Hope deferred makes the heart sick, but longing fulfilled is a tree of life.

Each step of our lives we go through changes, some huge, some minimal, some negative, some positive. We all face changes one time or another. To give oneself to Christ is a monumental change, one where we can gain a whole scope on life. Here one steps into a hope that our situations, our beings will take a different turn for the better. There is hope within this change.

But where do we find the rest of our hope?

This morning as I neared the downtown core, that question swirled in my head. Yes we find it in Christ, but that is too easy to say. Usually when we hope it is for material or short term things. Not to diminish those entities and not sound callous, should they be the objects that as Christians we should set our single focus on? Reflecting on Hebrews, Matthew's scriptures and the short saying of Linda Elerbee, I think of a small child's mind set, and how they embrace almost everything. Their innocence to accept and go along with, is more like a flowing tide then our hard biased state as adults. We struggle and analysis what Christ presents us. Yes, my hand is up for I am terrible for doing this.

However, when we put down our struggling against Him, then He is able to teach us what we need to know to survive the battles here on earth. As soon as we gave our lives to Christ we began a journey of change, each in our own individual ways. Step by step He has shaped us as a potter molds clay, to form what He envisioned in His mind of who we are in Him. It is more than that though. As we look beyond this very basic step into His world, He slowly lifts the veil so we may see more.

Where does our hope come from?

It comes from the Maker of Heaven & Earth. (Ps. 121:2)

It comes from God.

Acts 26:6 ".... the hope of the promise made of God..." Acts 26:7 "....... hoping to see fulfilled as they earnestly serve God day and night...." Romans 15:4 "For everything that was written in the past was written to teach us, so that through endurance and the encouragement of the Scriptures we might have hope."

It is a long term hope that generates the hope for everyday situations. It is the hope in the promises He has given to us through His word. This hope is truly the anchor of my soul, making my footsteps through life more steadfast upon Him our Saviour, our Protector.

Oh today may not seem like He is protecting us. I have many of those days & suppose may experience more ahead. Listen, we have made it this far, though! And even though you don't see it right now, it is a long way you have come from when you first believed.

When I departed home this morning I had a joy start to bubble up inside me, I questioned why it was there, for there was nothing exceptional that had happened that warranted it. But now I see there was, is the mere fact that I do have hope, even though if this or that does not work out. I have hope that He will make good on His promise that I will be with Him. The rest of my earthly days He has promised to be by my side, as well as yours, even when I must trek through muck

& mire, He is there. Even when I feel that He has abandoned me that is when He is carrying me.

'I BELIEVE IN TOMORROW & I WILL BE PART OF IT.'

It is amazing as I read this statement once more that an excitement rises in me. It is not that I believe in tomorrow for tomorrow's sake, it is that God has chosen me specifically, as He has chosen you, to experience this moment in time with Him.

I am part of what He has planned. What Joy, to know that I have been picked to be in this time of our history! There is where the hope is substantiated, in the fact that you have been chosen for this day. It is further perpetuated by His unwavering promises that He is with you, in all that you face. He has provided a solution, a way for you.

Thank Him for this day, for what He has made for you & ask Him what He would like you to learn, what you can do to sever Him, to whom would He like you to encourage this day.

May you be blessed.

Worth more than Sparrows – Feb 2/07

It was snowing out when I left the house for work.

Large white flakes covered my van like a soft blanket that sparkled in the gentle glow of the porch light. Sweeping it off was easy.

As I drove down the road I saw a large white rabbit bouncing towards me, he hopped over to the adjacent yard and sat there till I had past. The tips of his ears were beginning to turn brown; a sign that summer was coming. When? Well here in Calgary it could be any time between now and June.

How important we are to God. That is not a question. That is a statement. He values us greatly. This could be redundant to hear but we need to hear it, we need to have it soak down into our being as it becomes an engrained portion of us. There had been many things happening around us. This is the hour, to know that our Lord cares deeply for us. It will be challenged by the enemy, by others about us, even by our own mind.

Stand firm; be solid in the knowledge that Heavenly Father cares.

Our mind cannot comprehend at times how He could, and allow what is happening in our lives to happen.

Remember, He is far beyond our comprehension, even this portion of Him, the caring.

Father God you know the things that run through our mind, you know that they are subject to how we are personally feeling at the moment. They are affected by what we are experiencing. My request today, Father, that no matter what we are facing, no matter how large it is looming in front of us; that you would settle Holy Spirit, like the snow this morning, like a thick warm blanket over our shoulders. That it will be the first hour of many knowing, being washed by, soaking in Your deep loving care for us.

Amen
Be Blessed
Maggie

Matthew 16:26, For what is a man profited, if he shall gain the whole world, and lose his own soul? Or what shall a man give in exchange for his soul?

Living on Jan. 2/06

I read Genesis 5 this morning; yikes can you imagine living as long as some of those fellows did?

Noah was 500 when he had his sons.

When I was 30, I looked at my family history regarding length of life. On both sides I had grandparents that lived well into their 90's. Just recently an uncle & aunt celebrated their 90th birthdays. At 30 it meant

60 more years now it means 35 more years to get to my 90's. I have had a hard enough time dragging myself to this fine age of 55. We don't have to worry, the Lord has limited our years & we don't live over 100 in many cases.

What is living, how does one carry on after heart break upon heart break, not just to exist but to have quality life, as we see it?

One thought of it is changing our prospective on life.

Are we committing martyrdom if we settle for the life we have, or, woe is me, through the meager existence that at times we find ourselves in?

In a prophetic word that the Lord gave me on New Year's Day He said, "do not grow weary in your mundane tasks, but ask daily that My hand be diligently upon you….."

You know that I have experienced a lot of hard times. I could moan & groan & woe is me about it. But what kind of life is that? I have had numerous prophetic words through the years telling me of the "great" things I would be doing, but none have come about. In fact the complete opposite has happened. Those are the times when I had to honestly sit down with God & ask Him, "what is happening?" His reply was, "did you really say that?" In the majority of cases I had a perception of what He meant in His words. They were my perspectives, not His. When He talks about "wealth" we must be careful in knowing what wealth He is referring to. We can become disgruntled followers when He does not meet "our" expectations. In a way we set up ourselves for a fall, failure & disappointment when it was strength of character or faith He desired to build in us instead.

Once more this year, this time through my fiancé, the Lord gave me scriptures that He had given me before about my ministry. I could take it & run with it, like I did before, and misinterpreted it or worse put it in my human perspective, or, which I had chosen or let Him bring His word about in my life the way He had intended it to be.

I am living on with His truth.

I have heard of historical accounts that the great men & women of God were unassuming people of no great stature. Even our Lord Jesus Christ is described in the scriptures to be that way also. I have had the privilege to have met many men & women who serve the Lord, I am sad to say that most are arrogant & self-absorbed seeking after their own agenda. Yes they serve God; yes they have committed their lives to do so & do honour Him. But what else is present? Some have mansions to live in & ride around in huge chauffer driven cars & wave their arms in exclamation of Christ's benevolent nature when asking for funds to support their ministry.

But how does that help us put into perspective that path which He has put us on to walk?

"…….what shall a man give in exchange for his soul?"

There is nothing wrong with living in the blessings that Heavenly Father has given us, including financial. His followers live on every spectrum of society. However, if we set our sights on certain things, have we given something else up?

I did not intend to talk on such a topic as this. It seems though Heavenly Father had other ideas. I feel right now that He is encouraging us to focus or refocus on what we truly desire in our hearts, what are our aims & do they match up with His for us? Are we walking in His perspectives or our own? We can serve Him under our own concepts, but are they to the quality of what He desires us to have?

Boy, a lot of questions so early in the day, so early in the year.

I pray that the Lord our God, our Saviour Jesus Christ, and our comforter Holy Spirit move upon you. That His hand will be diligently upon your life. And that you will prosper in that which He has set out to bless you with.

God Bless
Maggie

Philippians 1:2-5 2:Grace and peace to you from God our Father and the Lord Jesus Christ. 3:I thank my God every time I remember you. 4:In all my prayers for all of you, I always pray with joy 5:because of your partnership in the gospel from the first day until now,

Being Thankful for one another Jan.3/07

The weather here has been quite beautiful. Our high yesterday was 11oC (51.8oF), but the Chinook wind was quite strong and as I sat @ a traffic light it swayed my van very noticeably. Like sitting in a covered rocking chair.

There was a cloth sale on at one of the fabric stores I visit. Yes I did buy some more, even though I have projects in various stages, waiting for me to complete plus lengths of some still yet to be cut. I like sewing and cannot quite keep up with what I have. I should go on another sewing blitz, one day just cutting out the material, another day sewing it together. I plan to take a couple more sewing courses as well.

Back to this morning where I am reminded of how thankful I should be for many things. We tend to get busy in our daily tasks and play, rarely stopping to think about one another. I do think of you on my e-mail list. Today reading another friend's email, whom I just added to my "stories" list, made me realize much more that there are others who read my stories. I thought of it, because she mentioned she was going to pass along my story to someone else. Of course being the analytical person that I am I have to question why I am thankful.

Are there particular aspects that I should be thankful for or just generally thankful?

Well it is rather simple, but profound just the same. I am thankful because if you were not here, I would not be who I am right now. Now for ones who have not met me could say, how could that be? If you were not reading this, then there would not be a need for Heavenly Father to encourage me to share what He has laid upon my heart. For those who have known me, recently or for a while, it is my interaction with you that has helped molded me to whom I am. You have helped in different ways to seek after Heavenly Father in a deeper way. Even just sitting down each morning asking Father for a scripture or what He is desiring me to share, has made me seek Christ in my life so I can be that vessel from which He can flow through. I have the same effect on you. If I did not send this to you or if it was not shared with you, then there would be topics that you may miss in contemplating and taking before the Lord.

Believe it or not I am thinking right now of my recent encounter with that American border guard. I should also be thankful for him having a brief snatch of time in my life. No it wasn't a pleasant encounter, but through it I have learned also, and God loves him as well. Therefore, he requires my prayers too.

Believe it or not I am finding this all intriguing to mull over. Specially the last thing about praying for that border guard. I must say that I was a thorn in his flesh at the time too, for I argued with him on some information that he had read to me, about me. It was wrong and I wasn't going to let that go. Mmmm… seems that I have a certain rapport with these guards. I will have to tell you the whole story(ies) if the Lord leads me to, another time.

One thing that I am thankful for with these guards is that they are there. They have a job to protect the borders from criminals etc. and I can imagine they put up with a lot more abuse then this little Canadian gal can dish out to them. I didn't really dish out abuse I just was determined in what I saw as being wrong. Even though they have hindered myself and others from getting married, or being together. They also stop terrorists as well as drug dealers from continuing on with their trades. So they may seem like bullies to us people who are honest and have no idea of other aspects of society, let alone living those lifestyles. I am thankful they are there and they are who they are.

I pray that "today, you will be touched by the hand of our Heavenly Father, that you will hear Christ's whisper in your ear of His love for you and feel the move of the Holy Spirit as He descends upon you. I am thankful for you. Thank you for being who you are and where you are in my life in this moment in time."

God Bless
Maggie

Exodus 4: 1 Moses answered, "What if they do not believe me or listen to me and say, 'The LORD did not appear to you'?" 2 Then the LORD said to him, "What is that in your hand?" "A staff," he replied.
What do you have on hand?

What do you have on hand? Jan.4/07

As I drove down Crowchild Trail towards the city center a brilliant crescent moon hung over the buildings. It's location in the sky made me quickly acknowledge that, even though we are still in winter, that spring was coming up fast.

It also reminded me of those romantic scenes in movie, where the sky is pitch black highlighted by the twinkling of building lights and stars, accompanied with a moon so bright that one can almost see the roundness of it rather than the light shard that is present to the eyes.

I spent the remainder of the time thanking Him for the love I have for Leroy & his for me, even more thankful for the love Christ has for me and His enabling me to return His love no matter how small it is.

I felt a peace settle into my spirit. My thoughts wandered and finally came to what He had said to me in a personal prophecy over the New Year, as many of you know I do struggle with what He asks of me… from time to time. Even though, my heart is still willing to complete His requests of me & so He has blessed me.

"What if they do not believe me or listen to me?" it is a comfort to know that such a man as Moses had similar thoughts. God's reply to him was simplistic as it is to all of us who venture the same enquiry… "What is that in your hand?"

To us there is a slight twist in both the question and answer. Today He asks "What do you have on hand?" Do we have a staff? Perhaps, but the shape is different, it is that of a man Jesus Christ not a piece of wood. The people of Israel and Egypt needed a visual sign that they could relate to, one that would stop the doubt of whether Moses heard from God or not.

We still require visual signs, but our relation points are different. We look for something that is a daily familiar sight, one where we know that it will not change substance or into another form unless it is by some miracle. And who is it that we know that does them more prolific then anything on earth? Our Lord Jesus Christ.

He knows the heart and mind of man, He knows what words or action it would take to shake them out of their unbelief into the reality of His existence. He is what we have on hand. Not for our purposes or like an everyday tool, it is because we had come to that pinnacle of realization and chose to follow Him, then we have become His tool. His tool to reach an unsaved world. We have Him on hand only due to this fact and only because He dwells in us.

1 John 4:13 Hereby know we that we dwell in him, and he in us, because he hath given us of his Spirit.

He has given us the most valuable tool one could ever have… His Spirit… Himself.

What do you have on hand today?

Psalm 109:21 - But you, O Sovereign LORD, deal well with me for your name's sake; out of the goodness of your love, deliver me

Much in love – Jan.10/07

I can't explain how I have been feeling these last 3 days. On Monday when I should have been recuperating, I was totally over the flu & very happy all day. At one point I stopped & asked Heavenly Father way was I feeling this way, excited?

His reply was quick & even brought up more joy in me; "You're in love – with Me!"

That is so true; I am a woman in love, in love with an awesome Bridegroom. That joy has lasted these past 3 days, even though my work load has increased & I received news that the oil company I work for wants to cut my hours to 3 days a week. Even though Leroy & I face odds with the US government in my visa. Even though... the list could go on.

Should not this love that has been imparted to us surmount all odds & not deter us from the woefulness that the enemy dumps upon us daily?

This love is not a fly by night one, it is not a star struck one where reason prevails, it is a sturdy well-grounded one, which returns itself in many ways I could not count.

What is my prayer today?

"Heavenly Father you moved upon me so that I could feel this incredible love inside me growing for you, I ask for a very special favour for all who read this that you move upon them the same way. That they would feel the love well up in them that they have for you. Cut through all the muck & grim that the enemy has smeared on them so they may rise up with not only healing but their love for you & your love for them, in their wings. So be it Lord."

Amen.

Hebrews 10: 26-31 (The Message) "If we give up and turn our backs on all we've learned, all we've been given, all the truth we now know, we repudiate Christ's sacrifice and are left on our own to face the Judgment—and a mighty fierce judgment it will be! If the penalty for breaking the law of Moses is physical death, what do you think will happen if you turn on God's Son, spit on the sacrifice that made you whole, and insult this most gracious Spirit? This is no light matter. God has warned us that he'll hold us to account and make us pay. He was quite explicit: "Vengeance is mine, and I won't overlook a thing" and "God will judge his people." Nobody's getting by with anything, believe me."

Arteries Clogged – Jan.12/07

On the way home last night via the 105 bus, we sometimes have to stop on one of the bridges that cross over the Bow River, due to the rush hour traffic. Yesterday was one of those days, as we waited I watched the river make its way through the slit opened in the ice crusted topping.

I remembered some winters where the river was so thick with ice that the force of its movement would buckle the dense layer, piling it up under the bridges & along the shores. It is called an ice flow. At times this ice flow can be quite hazardous as it piles up under the bridges clogging the river's every moving force.

I then thought of how cholesterol clogs our arties & hinders the flow of blood through them.

Same goes with all the little things that amount, one on top of another, in our lives affecting the flow between Heavenly Father & ourselves. Little things like not talking with Him daily or regularly, not reading His words to us in the scriptures regularly. Allowing our sensory perceptions to absorb things that are not of the Lord. Little things, things that may skip our thoughts or get way laid easily.

Sometimes before I fall asleep I tell the Lord I am too tired to have a conversation with Him. I know He understands the tiredness, but I also know that He waits eagerly for me to unfold my day to Him.

Sharing with Him how certain things made me feel or question why I reacted this way or that way when I wanted to respond differently. These missed or neglected things build up in the artery that we have between the Heavenly Throne & our earthly existence. After a while the walls are so thick the flow is threatened & in extreme cases may even be stopped.

"Heavenly Father my prayer request today is that you would inject more of your cleansing strength into us through Holy Spirit. Father clean out the artery that connects us with you so that your life flow is not hindered by the "little" things that collect in our lives. I thank you Heavenly Father that you first provided your Son Christ Jesus as our Saviour so that we could have that connection with you in a greater way, secondly Father thank you for Holy Spirit so that He will continually provide movement of you in our lives. Lord we need to have better heart health with you Father. I ask Lord that you will bless us with your grace & mercy in providing us with individual enlightenment so that we may obtain & maintain this. Thank you Lord. Thank you Father." Amen

Blessings,
Maggie

The Voice

Through the years many have asked me, "how do you know you're hearing God's voice and not your own or someone else's?"

I am not special in how I hear or know that I hear God's voice speaking to me. We all have had an experience of Him speaking to us, more than once. Before you came to know Jesus Christ as your personal Saviour, you heard God's voice speaking to your heart. As you have asked direction from time to time you have heard God's voice. To the why I hear as I do, I cannot totally say the why. I have spent years testing, to make sure that it was His voice, I have never stopped that testing. The depth of my gifting demands it. I have spent hours on my face or just sitting, listening. Always given a choice to if I want to do this or not. Taking the above scriptures literally, my desire was to recognize His voice when He calls, speaks, or sings. Did you know Heavenly Father sings over you? He does.

You may be asking me right now, what tests that I use, or have used to know it was or is Christ speaking to me. One is the scriptures. At the beginning, I would ask Him to speak through the scriptures to me, verifying that was Him. He did. But that is not full proof for the enemy also knows God's word, as we see in his attempt to dissuade Christ. But how is the scripture used? Is it to benefit only ourselves? Or is it used to Glorify our Creator and minister to others?

Secondly, I bounced off others what I had heard, asking them to inquire of the Lord if I was truly hearing correctly. Not just those friends who would say yes, but those I knew who would correct me.

Thirdly, bring it back. Sounds odd eh! But that is one of the tests I use, "Lord if this is of you then you bring it back to my mind when you desire." Surprisingly sometimes the thought I had, never returned. The words I had heard did return to my mind the following day, I would continue to quiz asking for insight.

Many have said if you can't find what He says to you in the scriptures then it is not Him. I have found that is not the case, there are many times He says things that I can't find in the scriptures, that is why I employed other means to test whether, or not, it is His voice. For instance, when I shared about Him calling me pretentious, can you find that in the scriptures? No, but was it God's voice? Yes, because He did it to make me stop, submit to correction and incorporate that correction into my life. It served a purpose; His glory was shown forth in the molding of me to be humble and a effective in my ministry to His children.

Why am I sharing about this today? To encourage you to take moments in the day to ask Heavenly Father to speak to you clearly. Write these down, test them. It is His voice that we should recognize when the enemy's comes, when the world comes, when our own self crowds in on us. We need to hear His voice to calm us, strengthen us, to encourage us. We are His sheep, it is His voice we should recognize above all others. Like a child knows their mother's or father's voice.

Psalm 34:4 "I prayed to the Lord and He answered me, freeing me from all my fears."

Be blessed today for you are His blessed child.

Ezra 3:11- "With praise and thanksgiving they sang to the LORD : He is good; his love to Israel endures forever." And all the people gave a great shout of praise to the LORD, because the foundation of the house of the LORD was laid."

EXPECTATIONS AND THANKFULNESS

This past little while nothing outside of the usual has happened on my bus trips. Yesterday I found myself quite tired and not sure if I really wanted to hear from the Lord Even when I am not faithful, He was faithful and spoke to me.

I felt that the Lord was talking about our expectations and thankfulness on our part. We all have expectations even though they haven't really formulated in our conscious thoughts yet. Like yesterday, riding on the # 1 bus, which is ten minutes before the #113, I was thinking about expectations. As riders on the bus we expect that the driver will drive safely enough to get us to our destination unharmed. As soon as we get off it and make our way to our own places of work, we expect that no one will hassle us on the way. Once there, our expectations are that the company is organized and proficient, so we may get our work done with minimal irritation.

Our expectations, what are they today? And what happens when they don't always work out the way we expect? Are we thankful to God for these irritants no matter what the size is?

I have not read Ezra often, it has been a couple of years since the last time. In a way, it seemed fresh to me to hear that the Israelites praised and thanked God in song.

Can we apply this verse to us today, in light of, what our unspoken or spoken expectations are?

May I paraphrase – "With praise and thanksgiving I sang to the Lord: "You are good, and your love to me endures forever." Even though my expectations of You go unmet, even though my expectations of other people are void. "I will give a great silent shout of praise to You, because the foundation of the house of my Lord was laid "… in my heart & in my life. So, when the sorrow & bewilderment besets me, I will stand firm on You, my God."

God's blessings on you today.

Aug 31

Finally Caught

I finally caught the elusive bus 113. I left much earlier today & could have caught the # 1 but people were already standing in it when it arrived at my stop so I opted out for the next bus that came along. And there it was… the 113. As I sat on one of the bench seats, I pondered about how different the atmosphere is on this one. There are more people who catch it & by the time it was half way DT people were standing in it. There also seemed to be a little social click going on as well…about 5-6 ladies all sat at the front & all knew each other…goes almost without saying the volume was a little more than the semi empty later 113 that I usually catch. There were others talking throughout the bus & the degree of the noise accentuated the fact of my almost hermit persona. But I won't reflect on that much today. Wow! Are you ever getting to know me! :-) That could be good or it could be bad.

I prayed for a scripture today during the commute & what came to mind was Nehemiah 5:12. Eagar to know what it said I looked it up before I started work, then reflected on how it would tie into my bus ride. I was puzzled, for I could think of a couple of topics; one is sort of a pet peeve of mine, in regards to the cost some of these Christian conferences are charging. But no, I won't go there either. Then a single word came to mind...differences...& I thought He was going to go into the direction of showing our differences. MMMM…...

Nehemiah 5:12 - "We will give it back, they said; And we will not demand anything more from them. We will do as you say." In Nehemiah 5, God is rebuking the Jews for extorting money from Jewish brothers, to the point of putting them into poverty. "How does this tie in, Lord, to my commute into the DT?" I thought I would leave it for a moment & put it aside & began to listen to the CD I was playing while I was working. "Who Am I" by Casting Crowns.

How inclusive we have made ourselves as Christians, in so many different ways. Through our denominations, our thoughts and beliefs, not feeling we want to go to church, including me in my reclusiveness. We are all different, not one of us has a full grasp on God's whole Truth.

I remember when I started my small craft company, CandyB Creates. I made decorative wreaths, among other things. Thinking it would be a good way to get a little extra money, I booked some craft fairs & tried to sell them on the side. It didn't work out very well. I pressed the Lord as to why. The answer I received was, "I gave you this talent for you to share with other people, not for profit." When I stepped into ministry & was beginning to do conferences & teachings etc., the Lord re-emphasized this topic. He gave me the prophetic gifting, yes it is up to me to keep it honed, but it is His gift for His use to bless others. Not for me to gain in profit or position. About 3 weeks ago I emailed a prophetic friend who has a worldwide stature, complaining about not being mentored by anyone while seeing others being mentored. I did not receive a reply back from my friend, as per usual, when I broached this question to other leaders in the prophetic. This always left me perplexed. But Father was faithful in responding. His reply was, as it has been over the years each time I have brought up the topic. "I will mentor you in My ways not in man's ways." Now one could say this is dangerous, for how would I know who I was hearing from? Interestingly enough, Father has provided people through my years of walking with Him to confirm & correct my thoughts. Yes, correct. Which brings me back to the topic…what is the topic? That is our differences & keeping things to ourselves. The Jewish people tried to do this, even to the extent of exploiting their own people. We see also in the NT when Jesus approached a Samaritan woman, how surprised she was that He, a proper Jew, would speak to her who was not a proper Jew. I have seen this in churches & Christian groups I have attended, even conferences where I have spoken & ministered. I was not talked to at first, for I was judged by my appearance (I was sometimes known as the lady in purple); then when realized that I was one of the speakers, attitudes changed & even more so after I spoke. My question has always remained, "why? Why do we do this?" Nehemiah 5:12 says, "don't demand anything." What do we demand of other Christians? It is not always money; it could be time, attention or other things. Do we have the right to do so? Is it exploitation to do so? When I am found out that I have a strong prophetic gifting I am often approached. I don't mind for this is a chance for me to bless others with what Father has given me (I don't have to go out on the limb by doing the approaching). But there are times when He will say, "I don't have anything for them right now." What an awkward position! I am all too aware of what rejection they may feel. The first time faced with that I pressed God with a "diplomatic" way to present it. I am Canadian after all & we are a diplomatic people. He gave me this, "At present Father has not given me anything for you, however, He does desire to speak with you & I suggest that you pray & ask if He would like to speak with you directly or through someone else or both." Then I say a blessing over them. Our exclusivity robs us of being blessed & robs others from being blessed by what Father has given to us to bless others with. (Yes, Leroy I hear you – my fiancé does lecture me too). It could be a person on the street or your closest friend or any number of people in between, Christian or non, Jew or Gentile.

Romans 12:16-21

"16 Live in harmony with one another. Do not be proud, but be willing to associate with people of low position. Do not be conceited. 17 Do not repay anyone evil for evil. Be careful to do what is right in the eyes of everybody. 18 If it is possible, as far as it depends on you, live at peace with everyone. 19 Do not take revenge, my friends, but leave room for God's wrath, for it is written: "It is mine to avenge; I will repay," says the Lord. 20 On the contrary: "If your enemy is hungry, feed him; if he is thirsty, give him something to drink. In doing this, you will heap burning coals on his head." 21 Do not be overcome by evil, but overcome evil with good."

HARMONY, NOT DEFEAT

Have you ever walked in your sleep? I think that is how I felt this morning as I trudged down to the bus stop. But I caught the elusive bus #113, for the second day in a row. It wasn't as busy as it was yesterday, which was nice especially when sleepy.

Upon rising, I asked Heavenly Father what scripture He had for today, on the bus He blessed me with the insight to read Romans 12:16-21. When I got to work, I was acutely aware how fortunate I am to be able to listen to my Christian radio station. I work by myself in the well file room so there is no one to disturb, I play the radio at a low volume so no offices around are disturbed. When someone does come in and desires a conversation I turn the music off. That awareness brought about a song in my head… you know the one… "Thank you, Thank you" …dum dum dum… you know the one… chuckle. One of those tunes that goes around in your head but asked to hum a few bars or sing the words you can't. It perked me up though. I read the scripture and quizzing the Lord to what He would like to highlight or share for today.

I would have to say, personally, this is one of the harder scriptures to incorporate into one's life. For each person looks at things differently. At one church, I attended I was the prophetic group leader and an elder, as well as a home group leader. A friend of mine at the time who was brought up in a Christian home, began to get upset with me. She began to taunt me, coercing others to do the same. I went into prayer about this, for the incidents were escalating and becoming more overt. I would have to say that I was not equipped to handle such things from a friend of many years. I decided to end our friendship. When in church I would greet her, but would not hold a conversation with her nor spend time with her like we had in the past. She began to spread rumors around the church until one of the group's members approached me to let me know what was happening. My friend and I finally did have a talk where I explained my sorrow and she explained hers. What it boiled down to was she was jealous for I had been quickly accepted into the church community and placed into leadership, where when she came a year after me she was not. She apologized and I accepted and forgave her, but declined the renewal of our friendship to the level that it had been. Her reaction was to go to the pastor. I was called into his office one Sunday after services along with my friend and someone she chose to bring. Each of us gave our side of the situation. My pastor asked me to renew the friendship, and when I declined, he suggested that I step down from leadership if I could not forgive the lady. I explained that I had forgiven her, but in doing so it did not mean that I had to renew the friendship to where it was because trust had been broken. More so when rumors that had been spread by her were based on those things we had shared in confidence with each other. I directed some questions to the lady, "had I ever snubbed you when you came to church? Had I ever been rude to you? "When she answered no, then I added, "and so it will be as this, we are acquaintances, but not close friends as before." The pastor back tracked on his decision to have me step down from leadership. I will concede that I could have handled the situation a little differently, but at the time this is how I did it.

Verse 16 "Live in harmony with one another…"

I chose to live in harmony to the best of my ability, but even to today that view of harmony is not always shared in return.

Verse 17 "Do not repay anyone evil for evil. Be careful to do what is right in the eyes of everybody."

We should pressure the Lord for what is right in His eyes first. Sometimes our flesh will fight against what He will say. For instance, repenting for something we did not do. My son told his wife once that I had abandoned him when he was a child. When I heard that I was bothered, beyond belief, that he would even think that, for I hadn't. I bugged God greatly on it, His reply, "It doesn't matter if you did or didn't. He thinks you did, therefore, repent for it. In doing so you take the ground of accusation in that area away from the enemy." I went into repentance asking for Jesus to guide me.

Verse 19 "Do not take revenge"

It is easy to want to take revenge, it can be intricately complex or as simple as spreading of rumors on the person who started to spread ones about you. It is a fine balance to not be revengeful, it doesn't mean we lay down and take the guff. No, but how we respond is very important. Notice I said respond, not react. People may think we are pushovers if we do not react quickly as they would. Contemplating your response in prayer can be more damaging to the enemy's advance on your life.

Verse 20, is it taking it a step too far, especially when someone has hurt you, or so our minds would want us to believe. Yes, it takes a lot of God's power in our will to not only do it but do it with a proper attitude. If my ex-friend came today and knocked on my door asking for food, I would gladly give it to her and then some. If my son came to me today and requested my time and attention, I would clear my slate for him. But most of all I would want to do it with all the love Christ could flow through me.

Verse 21 "Do not be overcome by evil, but overcome evil with good."

We are to be overcomers in this earthly world, we are to be the victors.

Circumstances can seem to be too much for us to hold onto this fact that we are already overcomers. That fact is at our disposal, it is in our arsenal, it is our weapon to rise up and be the victors Christ has created us to be. Seek the Lord for Him to aid you in incorporating this into your life.

Blessings of being an overcomer, living in harmony as the Lord shows you.

Song - Thank you, Lord by Don Moen,

«To hear You say, ‹this one›s Mine›…. Now I am spoken for."
Song by Mercy Me –cd Spoken For

IT'S IN THE MIND part one

Ephesians 3:6-10 "6 This mystery is that through the gospel the Gentiles are heirs together with Israel, members together of one body, and sharers together in the promise in Christ Jesus. 7 I became a servant of this gospel by the gift of God's grace given me, through the working of His power. 8 Although I am less than the least of all God's people, this grace was given me: to preach to the Gentiles the unsearchable riches of Christ 9 And to make plain to everyone the administration of this mystery, which for ages past was kept hidden in God, who created all things. 10 His intent was that now, through the church, the manifold wisdom of God should be made known to the rulers and authorities in the heavenly realms"

I thought Heavenly Father was going to share about another topic today but on the way to the bus He didn't say anything. Near my DT stop I asked the Lord if I could have a scripture to read. Ephesians 3 was the one He encouraged me to read. At work, I looked it up and enjoyed reading it. Later, I asked what He would like to share on the topic in the verses. He said read over the scripture and highlight the parts that stand out. During my break, I did. He said, "what was the topic yesterday?" It was on renewing our minds. Reread the highlighted sections of the Bible passage.... "Sharers together in the promise in Christ Jesus.... the gift of God's grace...unsearchable riches of Christ...administration of this mystery.... was hidden in God.... The manifold wisdom of God should be made known..." Yesterday's scripture was, Romans 12:2 ".... Then you will be able to test and approve what God's will is—His good, pleasing and perfect will."

I find it interesting how God lays the beginning of something then builds on it. Yesterday, He desired us to remember we must renew our minds, so that today we may grasp the portions of scripture He desires us to understand. Perhaps, see it in a new light but maybe in a deeper depth.

I thought of the trouble in the Middle East with Israel and listen to the news reports I noticed how the reports are slighted. I don't believe in war nor that Israel is justified in what they are doing. But it is part of the prophesies to come. When people say to me, pray for peace in Israel, I seek God first – What type of peace? In light of today's scriptures, I see it is Christ's peace. Peace of mind in the fellowshipping with the Only Living God, Yahweh. This is the promise we share with the Israelites. The riches of Christ are so vast we can not comprehend it all, nor a portion and defiantly not without a renewed mind. I feel a slight sensation of awe. A mystery He has hidden in Himself until this time, we are indeed privileged to live now to see it revealed. How peculiar and wonderful to know that He has created us for this time, so we may see His revelation. A God, who knew us from the beginning of time, chose now for us to be witnesses of what He is doing. I do not want to miss any of it, "so please, Lord, renew my mind in Christ so I can understand Your wisdom as You desire us to come to know it. Thank you, Father.

Lord what an honor to be able to serve You and fellowship with You in this day. Let us be ever so thankful Lord, with continuous praises on our lips for You. Bless us this day, Lord. Thank you, Father. Amen.

It is not often that the Lord will continue a story to the next day, in this case He did.

It's in the Mind part two

Romans 5:1 ss - "Therefore, since we have been justified through faith, we have peace with God through our Lord Jesus Christ."

Romans 5:10 –"For if, when we were God's enemies, we were reconciled to Him through the death of His Son, how much more, having been reconciled, shall we be saved through His life!"

I woke up to my 5am alarm with two scriptures in mind, Romans. 5:1 and 10. I read them before I dozed off for another half hour. I set my alarm several times for the morning because I am a very deep sleeper and must wake up in stages. At 5am the Scriptures really didn't mean much to me. I felt to expound on the other topic from yesterday, When I read the scriptures earlier I did not see the significance of them. Now, rereading them, I do.

Jesus desires us to renew our mind in Him so we can see the Truth of Him as well as things through Him. I feel He also desires to re-emphasize the fact that it is through Him.

"We have been justified through faith".

It is His faith that He gives us, so that we may have faith in Him. Without it, as well as, without the renewing of our mind to see this, we cannot ascertain the type of faith that will sustain us through the battles we must face. With this faith, we have a peace that does astound, not only our enemies, but ourselves. Peace in Him, the Peace of Christ. Without this peace, we can ascertain that which is His good, pleasing, and perfect will. Without the renewing of our mind, we do conform to this world, for there is no sense in us to see or do things any other way. In this state, we are enemies of God, as He says in verse 10, for we do not have Him in our sights or heart. God took the steps to reconcile us to Himself. He provided the means to be reconciled, who is Christ. Now, He tells us the means by which we can be reconciled, but comprehend that state and stay in it. This is the renewing of our mind.

"How much work you have done for us, Lord. How intricate each step is so that we may come to know You. Father, once again, I come to ask that You renew our minds so that we do not have conflict with You, only with the enemy of both You and ourselves. You reconciled us to Yourself through Your Son, Christ so that we could kneel under Your saving grace. But You did not stop there, Lord. You have continued on, with the desire that we may be able to fellowship with You. That being the state of renewing our minds through You and in You. We are truly justified by faith, Your Faith, not our own. How great and wonderful you are, Lord.

Father, is there any portion of our minds today that has not been renewed by You? I ask as a favor for myself and my friends, that You would draw us close, to do that renewing so that we can have total reconciliation and not be at odds with You. Thank you, Father. Bless us with the Peace of Christ, Lord." Amen

Dieu vous aime – God loves you

PASSED THROUGH

This is a day to greet Heavenly Father with a joyful hello and thank Him for His son Jesus Christ and our comforter Holy Spirit.

No, I don't wake up this way. I wake up with a tight time frame with one purpose in mind, please don't expect a conversation and don't get in my way.

I can't believe it, there is something about me and this catching the earlier bus #113. I knew I was going to be a little late so I didn't bother rushing. Sure enough, as I ended the back alley, to head to the main street, the #113 comes along. No, I don't run for buses. It sat at the stop like it always does till I reached the corner to cross. That is when he decides to leave. If I was paranoid I would say he does that on purpose, but I am not paranoid. Or as Data from Star Trek would say, "I am not paranoid, just an annoyed android." Anyhow, caught the #1 which came next. As I sat on the bus looking out the window what came to mind was Matthew 25:1-14 about the ten virgins. I thought about how the first one in line, going through the door must have felt. Then about the last one going through the door. It reminded me of a prophetic insight I had once had about the five virgins who stayed and were able to step through the door. I saw the five in this prophetic insight, holding their lanterns high as they made their way up a slope to a small door in the side of a large fortress wall. A man stepped out of the door who stood part in the opening, in it, in order to keep the heavy wooden door from slamming shut. I don't know why he didn't stand inside to hold it; that would have been more logical. Nonetheless, that is what he did. Each virgin passed through the opening, stooping slightly to clear the header. When it came to the last one, I saw that it was me in that position. I can remember, looking into the man's eyes as I slipped passed him. He had the look of one about to scold you, my impression was, "you're lucky you made it." I felt that was us here in these last days, however long that will be, we have narrowly slipped passed the one who holds the door open so that we can go in and meet the bridegroom. What joy to be in that group, no matter whether it is first or last. What an awesome privilege to meet the Bridegroom. I don't want to be one of the five virgins who had to go back to buy some oil. Would they had or will they experience the same sensation I do when the 113 comes by, sits just long enough then leaves seconds before I can make it across the street to catch it.

Is there another bus coming?

Will He give the five virgins who didn't have enough oil in their lamps another chance?

I don't know, I don't see that in the scriptures.

What I feel He is telling us is be prepared, soak in His presence now, get to know Him now, be filled to the brim with Him now, no matter what you are facing today. For we do not know the hour in which He may come. Already, Father God has to hold back His Son from His Bride because she is still preparing herself. Let us, friends, prepare today for the greeting of our Bridegroom, He is coming, it is inevitable.

Sing your new song today, seek Him in the morning, at noon, in the evening, whenever, wherever.

Rejoice in the fact that He is still present with us, but know that the day grows shorter. Draw nigh to Him & He will draw nigh to you.

Blessing you this day.

RENEWING OUR MINDS

Romans 12:2 KJV 2 And be not conformed to this world: but be ye transformed by the renewing of your mind, that ye may prove what is that good, and acceptable, and perfect, will of God.

Romans 12:2 NIV 2 Do not conform any longer to the pattern of this world, but be transformed by the renewing of your mind. Then you will be able to test and approve what God's will is—His good, pleasing and perfect will.

I had an uneventful bus ride this morning, my thoughts kept coming back to what was going through my mind this weekend. I began to write some of it down then put it away, yet for it to come back this morning. Often in sermons we have heard references made to the "battle" that is in our minds. That is where the enemy tests us the most. When I was a child I often had depressions. Even though they said I was a manic depressive, no prescription was given. This continued into my teens. When my first husband left my children and myself, I went into a deep depression losing two months of time. I was given no medication to help me through that time period. When my children were about seven or eight I had another bad bout. This time, I was given medication which I hated the side effects, so stopped taking it. I was a new Christian and was struggling with how I could serve the Lord. I confronted Him one day, "How do You expect me to do anything for You when I find it difficult to handle things day to day?"

"And be not conformed to this world:"

Slowly, "that fog" began to lift. For the first time in my life, I could think clearly. Was that the end of depression? No, but the cloud was gone. There was one big session after that. I had wanted a career and was taking night school. I hit a brick wall, mentally and emotionally, taking three months sick leave. I didn't feel – mentally – depressed but my physical symptoms showed I was. My company suggested I go to a physiologist. I did, a Christian one, towards the end of the 3 months. I pressed the Lord to tell me why I was going through this and what to do now. His only response was –"They (company – the work force) wants your soul, don't give it to them."

"Do not conform any longer to the pattern of this world, but be transformed by the renewing of your mind."

As a younger Christian, I had heard this scripture in Romans, plus quoting it to myself, often. I sought after its meaning. Over the years, I have heard of the mind battle ground, watching fellow believers fall because of the mental struggles they had encountered. Am I infallible, not likely for I still have many struggles myself. It has only been these recent months that I have learned to push past the opposition that strives to bring me down.

In December 2006, it was extremely difficult, I found myself staying in bed for days at a time. God, in His mercy, drew me out to look once more beyond that which enshrouded me. I was without hope. I felt that was my worst test, not realizing something far worse was to come. He pulled and pulled and I pushed to get into the renewed mind that we are supposed to have.

Do not conform… do not see things as the world sees them. For that sight is limited, without hope, it traps us in despair. Rather, lend your mind, no give, no sacrifice your mind over to Christ, so He can renew them.

My hope is in Him…even though I go through the shadow of the valley of death… I will fear no evil, for my mind has been renewed. Forgive me for melding the Scriptures together but it is for a point. I could lose my faith if I would give into what the enemy whispers in my mind about God. The battle rages, the enemy says "God does not love me, therefore no one loves me; God has abandoned me, therefore everyone has abandoned me; God does not let anything good happen in my life therefore, my life is worthless."

If I have conformed to that which the world sets their eyes upon. Bitterness and sorrow will beset me and I become not of Him who is gracious, full of love. Once more, I must lift my mind up to the Creator of Heaven and Earth asking, "Renew my mind, wash it, cleanse it." Then will I be able to test and approve what God's will is—His good, pleasing and perfect will. It is then I will be able to see through His eyes and respond as He responds. It is then, I will know His Truth.

The battle rages in the mind. Seize it this day and take it to the Lord, for in that renewing of our He will give you the weapons, not only to halt the enemy, but to end his advancement on your mind.

What do you know as Truth? – "God so loved the world that He <u>gave</u> His only begotten Son, so they may not perish but have everlasting life."

Take hold of your mind, no matter what has beset you, take hold of it with force giving it to the Lord to renew it.

"Heavenly Father, You know what each one of us are going through right now, our weak spots that would allow our mind to conform to the world's concepts. You know so well how the battle rages in our minds. Aid us Lord, for we are weak people. Aid us to give our minds to You to be renewed so we may stand up and take back that which the enemy has taken in our thoughts. Take our tainted concepts, Lord, renew our mind so these concepts become Yours. To see how You see, to respond how You would respond. We are imperfect beings, but, yet You created in us perfection and so lovingly gave us perfection so we may know Your will and follow You with Your love and devotion. Thank you, Father, that you meet us where we are today.

Amen

SING

It has been a while since I shared. Not much in regard to bus stories, but Heavenly Father is faithful in speaking to me in the mornings. I was ill the first part of the week but feel better now.

This morning, as I sat on the early 105 bus to work, I asked Heavenly Father what He would like to share. Psalm 89 came to my mind first, then Psalm 98. At work, I had a few minutes to read both Psalms. I smiled at what they had to say. When checking my email, I looked at one of the online newsletters I get. It had an article about feeling and looking better. My thoughts returned to the first two verses in each of the Psalms I had just read.

Psalm 89:1- "I will sing of the LORD's great love forever; with my mouth, I will make Your faithfulness known through all generations."

Psalm 98:1- "Sing to the LORD a new song, for He has done marvelous things; His right hand and His holy arm have worked salvation for him."

How can we sing a song, let alone a new one, of His faithfulness, if we lack joy? Let not your countenance be downcast. In verse three of Psalm 98 it says "He has remembered his love and his faithfulness to the house of Israel; all the ends of the earth have seen the salvation of our God."

He remembered His love and His faithfulness to the house of Israel. We are part of that house, for we have been grafted into the vine. As much as He remembers His love for Israel, so He remembers His love for us personally, today. The enemy attacks our thoughts, trying to tell us that God has forgotten us, He doesn't love us, and He's not faithful. Thus, a spark of joy departs. My friends what do we have in our possession to counteract this attack and regain our joy?

SING. There are different methods of song; they can start merely by saying words or a full outburst of melody.

Hebrews 12:1-13

1 Therefore, since we are surrounded by such a great cloud of witnesses, let us throw off everything that hinders and the sin that so easily entangles. And let us run with perseverance the race marked out for us, 2 fixing our eyes on Jesus, the pioneer and perfecter of faith. For the joy set before him he endured the cross, scorning its shame, and sat down at the right hand of the throne of God. 3 Consider him who endured such opposition from sinners, so that you will not grow weary and lose heart. God Disciplines His Children 4 In your struggle against sin, you have not yet resisted to the point of shedding your blood. 5 And have you completely forgotten this word of encouragement that addresses you as a father addresses his son? It says, "My son, do not make light of the Lord's discipline, and do not lose heart when he rebukes you,6 because the Lord disciplines the one he loves, and he chastens everyone he accepts as his son." 7 Endure hardship as discipline; God is treating you as

his children. For what children are not disciplined by their father? [8] If you are not disciplined—and everyone undergoes discipline—then you are not legitimate, not true sons and daughters at all. [9] Moreover, we have all had human fathers who disciplined us and we respected them for it. How much more should we submit to the Father of spirits and live! [10] They disciplined us for a little while as they thought best; but God disciplines us for our good, in order that we may share in his holiness. [11] No discipline seems pleasant at the time, but painful. Later on, however, it produces a harvest of righteousness and peace for those who have been trained by it. [12] Therefore, strengthen your feeble arms and weak knees. [13] "Make level paths for your feet," so that the lame may not be disabled, but rather healed.

VIEWING DISCIPLNE

I woke up at 4:30am from a dream, in a semi- conscious state the Lord laid Hebrews 12 on my heart. I wanted to just roll over and go back to sleep. Tried, it didn't work. I got up and to read the Scripture. Reading the first two verses I then tried to sleep again till my alarm went off. Silly me. I went online and printed the scripture off to read at work. I caught the earlier 113 bus. Once in the office I was able to read the whole passage before the work day began. I was inspired, by the Lord, to view discipline in a different way, in His Light.

Some people view discipline as being punishment by a mean overseer. In some cases, that is true, where the overseer desires only to inflict their control. But done by a parent, teacher, so forth, the ones who can see the potential in a person. The ones who wish in their own heart to see the other person grow and flourish, then it is done in love. Dr. Dobson, a Christian psychologist calls it tough love. God inflicts the same type of discipline on us, discipline of Love. It is hard not to look at the negative of discipline. The latter portion of verse 5 says – "and do not lose heart when He rebukes you," and the first portion of verse six "because the Lord disciplines those He loves," The writer of Hebrews goes onto say that we are His sons/daughters, thus He treats us as such. ".... but God disciplines us for our good.... "verse ten.

What is "the reason," for His disciplining us? That we may share in "His holiness." Without a renewed mind, I feel that we would not be able to understand this aspect and therefore would miss out on any blessings He wishes to bestow upon us. Part of those blessings are expressed in verse 11 "...it produces a harvest of righteousness and peace for those who have been trained by it." Not a cupful, nor a bucketful, but a harvest. No, it is not pleasant being disciplined. I know, for there has been a few times .... Oh, ok many times... where I have had my ears flicked by Heavenly Father. And have had my gifting (the prophetic) removed because I wasn't handling it properly. It is also, my testimony that there was a harvest of peace afterwards the discipline. Peace of heart, peace of mind, in knowing God loves me that much to continually being observant of me and correcting me. I feel closer to Him for it is another aspect of His love. His arms of correction are also extended to draw us near to His heart.

What an encouragement verses 12 and 13 are: "12 Therefore, strengthen your feeble arms and weak knees. 13 Make level paths for your feet so that the lame may not be disabled, but rather healed." His strengthening, to even realize that healing comes through His discipline. We are no longer lamed by our sin and rebelliousness, which cripples our walk with Christ.

"Father, thank you. Thank you for Your discipline. Move upon us, Jesus, to renew our minds in the area of God's disciplining of us. Let us not chaff against it, but embrace it knowing it is in Your love and good will that do it. Open our eyes to Your motion in this regard so we do not mistake it for the enemy's tricks, thus pushing it away. But make us wise in the choice to accept Your rebuke, asking to learn from it. Thank you, Father. Amen.

CPSIA information can be obtained
at www.ICGtesting.com
Printed in the USA
BVHW071201190819
556214BV00004B/428/P

9 781728 322483